His Dangerous Bride

By Merry Farmer

HIS DANGEROUS BRIDE

Copyright ©2015 by Merry Farmer

Paperback Edition

This book is a work of fiction. Names, characters, places, and incidents are products of the author's imagination or are used fictitiously. Any resemblance to actual events or locales or persons, living or dead, is entirely coincidental.

Cover design by Erin Dameron-Hill (the miracle-worker)
Embellishment by © Olgasha l Dreamstime.com

ASIN: B01ADVLOIW
Paperback:
ISBN-13: 978-1523302154
ISBN-10: 1523302151

If you'd like to be the first to learn about when the next books in the series come out and more, please sign up for my newsletter here: http://eepurl.com/RQ-KX

Like historical western romance? Come join us in the Pioneer Hearts group on Facebook for games, prizes, exclusive content, and first looks at the latest releases of your favorite historical western authors. https://www.facebook.com/groups/pioneerhearts/

A year ago, I waved goodbye to Corporate America and joined the ranks of the full-time authors.

It was kinda like accepting an offer to be a mail-order bride.

Good thing it worked out!

Table of Contents

Chapter One

Haskell, Wyoming – 1875

Like most saloon fights, it started with alcohol and a bad attitude. The Paradise Ranch boys would argue later that they were just there to enjoy a pleasant evening of cards in the company of the girls from Bonnie's place across the way. They had *no idea* that Rex Bonneville's rough and tumble employees would be there too, celebrating the deal Bonneville had just signed giving them an exclusive contract with the beef distributor who owned the stockyard closest to Haskell. Sure, the Paradise Ranch boys were a bit put out that this deal meant they would have to drive their cattle a hundred miles to the stockyard in Culpepper until Howard Haskell could sort things out, but honestly, they were just there to play cards and flirt with the ladies. Honestly.

And while, yes, Luke Chance's declaration that "Only a lily-livered, slack-jawed, bone-headed coward would hide behind a piece of paper in the face of a little competition" was said as a means of constructive criticism, it caused one of Bonneville's thugs—that is, his employees—Stavros "The Greek" Papadopoulos, to throw a hard-knuckled punch right at Luke's face. The resounding crack of fist hitting bone rang throughout the saloon. Moments later, chairs clattered to the floor and glass shattered as bottles were chucked aside, tables overturned, and the boys went at each other.

Luke had never been one to back down from a little mayhem—not when he was a boy picking pockets to help his parents put food on the table for him and his three siblings, not when his parents died and he had to protect Libby, Freddy, and Muriel after they were sent to the orphanage, and not when they made the journey west on the Oregon Trail ten years ago. He leapt over splintered chairs to thump Stavros, giving as good as he got. He wrenched a leg free from a crushed table and proceeded to use it as a bat to defend his mates as the brawl spread to the dais Bonnie's girls used to kick up their skirts to raucous music, like the ladies did in France. And he rushed to protect those girls when half of Bonneville's toughs pulled out pistols that should have been confiscated before they entered the saloon.

After that, it was over before anyone could holler boo—or get shot, thankfully. Luke was left with a shiner that stung like the dickens as sweet Pearl Pettigrew dabbed a cool, wet cloth on it, and a vicious ache in his side where a chair had been smashed into him. The saloon had been torn to shreds in a matter of minutes, and both Bonneville's crew and the boys of Paradise Ranch learned what real fear was when the barkeep, Sam Standish, the saloon's owner, Charlie Garrett, and Haskell's sheriff, Trey Knighton, took charge of the scene with a vengeance.

That was how Luke—and a dozen other men—ended up spending the night in Haskell's cramped jail. It was why Howard Haskell was in a foul mood when he came to bail out half his ranch hands. It was also why Luke was seen leaving Bonnie's place at nine in the morning, his clothes in disarray, his lips red, and his left eye swollen shut. But it wasn't what it looked like.

"Franklin!" Luke winced as he hopped off the stoop in front of Bonnie's and flagged down his supervisor on the ranch. "Hey, Franklin, hold up a second."

A few steps ahead, Franklin Haskell, with his pretty, new wife, Corva, on his arm, stopped and glanced back over his shoulder. He jolted in shock at the sight of Luke rushing toward him. Luke couldn't fight the grimace that his fresh injuries brought to his face. He'd seen worse after being bucked by a horse or kicked by an irate heifer, but not all at once. He wiped his grimy forehead with the back of his hand, wishing the jail had a bucket of water at least for a bath, and came to a stop in front of Franklin and Corva.

"Morning, ma'am." He nodded to Corva—whose mouth hung open as she took in the sight of him and the building he'd just come out of—then turned to Franklin. "So, boss, some of the boys and I were talking last night about how we have to drive the herd all the way to the stockyard in Culpepper next month because of Bonneville's sneaky deal."

Franklin's shock stiffened to a frown. He stood straighter, hugging his wife's arm, as if to protect her from a madman. "Yes. It's unfortunate, but true."

Luke nodded, widening his stance and planting his hands on his hips. He gave Franklin his most winning smile and said, "Well, boss, I'd like a chance to lead that drive."

Silence followed. Franklin stared at him, sweeping him with a look that said more than any words could, and none of it good. He cleared his throat. "Have you seen a doctor about your eye?"

Luke winced, which didn't help the pain radiating from the eye in question. "Sam made sure Doc Milligan tended to all the boys in lock-up last…" He let his words fade to nothing, then cleared his throat. "I should probably explain what happened last night." Bad as it was, and as hard as it would be to explain, a wily grin tickled Luke's lips.

Franklin exchanged a glance with his wife, then both of them turned to Luke with varying degrees of reproof.

"I know what happened last night," Franklin said. "Dad told me all about it before he rode out here to pay your bail. Travis Montrose is back at the ranch, trying to do your work and his while he waits for you lot to get home."

"I wouldn't want to face him if he's still in the mood he was first thing this morning," Corva added.

Luke ran a hand over his sore jaw, dreading what he couldn't avoid. At least he would face it with Cody and Mason and a few others. Right now, he had other things to worry about.

"All right. Admittedly, none of this looks good. But just because of one saloon fight—in which we were all defending the honor of Paradise Ranch and your family, I should add—it doesn't mean we shouldn't be thinking about business and the future." He shifted his weight, his pulse ratchetting up as he got ready to frame his argument. "I've been working on the ranch for almost ten years now. I know cattle and wrangling better than I know anything else. If we have to drive the herd a hundred miles to get them to the stockyard, then so be it. But I want to be the one who leads that drive. I know I can do it."

His bid for a leadership role was met by a hard look from Franklin. Prickles of uncertainty raced down Luke's back. Dammit, he knew that he was capable of leading a cattle drive. He was capable of a lot more responsibility than he had on the ranch. If only there was a way to prove he was responsible, that he was a leader.

"Yoo-hoo, Luke!"

Pearl's sugary call from an upper window in Bonnie's place sent a zip of dread down Luke's spine. Nothing shot a speech like the one he'd just made in the foot faster than a whore waving from an upstairs window of a cathouse. Trying not to wince, Luke twisted to look up and wave back to her.

Pearl stood with her elbows resting on the window frame, a position which pushed her ample bosom dangerously close to spilling right out of the top of her corset. She already had lip-rouge on, and her curly hair hung loose in a tempting mass around her porcelain shoulders. Not exactly the image you wanted your boss to see.

"Della says I just missed you," Pearl said, a bright smile on her face. "She said you stopped by to make sure us girls were all right after the kerfuffle last night."

"Yep," Luke said, the grimace in his voice, if not on his face.

"He's such a nice man," Pearl called down to Franklin and Corva. "So kind and considerate of us girls. And so handsome too. Why, half the time we've got a mind to entertain him free of charge."

Luke burst into an awkward laugh. "Gee, thanks, Pearl." He snuck a peek at Franklin and Corva. Corva was every bit as scandalized as Luke had worried she'd be, but Franklin's expression had gone as blank as stone, which was worse. "I don't actually patronize Bonnie's girls,"

Luke tried to make light of things. "Never even considered it," he added in a mutter, blushing at the little lie.

"I just wanted to let you know that I'm okay too," Pearl continued from above. "I feel more sorry for all you boys. It was such a shame you all got arrested. But Mr. Garrett was saying that he'd find a way to put a stop to all your excess energy if he had to drag every woman at Hurst Home out here to Haskell personally, whatever that means."

Twin pricks of horror and hope ricocheted through Luke's chest. His adopted mother, Josephine Evans, was one of the ladies who had been involved in bringing Corva Haskell out to Wyoming as a mail-order bride for Franklin. She and Franklin's aunt, Virginia Piedmont, and Charlie Garrett had taken on the task of helping the unfortunate women who found themselves as Hurst Home—a safe haven in Nashville, Tennessee for women who had been abused or otherwise found themselves in danger—to find husbands here in Haskell. Ever since Franklin had started smiling again and telling everyone how happy he was with Corva and how in love, Josephine had been pestering Luke to let her find a bride for him too.

Above them, Pearl uttered a surprised squeak, then ducked her head into her room. A second later, she reemerged to say, "I gotta go do my chores now. Miss Bonnie says a clean house is a safe house. And Doc Milligan is coming later for our monthly check-ups. Maybe you could come by after?" She gave him her sweetest smile and batted her eyelashes at him.

Luke flushed hot and cold. He cleared his throat and checked to see what Franklin and Corva thought. Not much of him, if their expressions were any indication. "We'll see," he called up to Pearl.

She blew him a kiss, then ducked back into her room.

Luke rubbed the back of his neck, and shifted to flash a sheepish grin Franklin's way. "Bonnie's girls can be a little overfriendly." He took a step closer to Franklin and Corva and squared his shoulders. "Bonnie's girls aside, I know I can lead that cattle drive. I know I'm capable of far more than I've been doing on the ranch."

"You're a hard worker," Franklin admitted, his eyes narrowed in consideration.

"Yes, sir, I am." Luke nodded. "Let me prove that to you."

Franklin let out a breath and shook his head. "Saloon fights? Bonnie's girls? Not to mention the hoopla you and Cody Montrose caused earlier in the summer when you bought that jug of Silas Purdue's moonshine."

Luke burst into a chuckle before he could stop himself. That had been a night and a half—something he and Cody would be talking about for years to come. But right now, it wasn't what he wanted his boss thinking about.

"I swear, I'm ready to turn over a new leaf, to leave my misspent youth behind me," he insisted. "I'm getting too old for those antics anyhow. I want something real— real responsibility and a future."

"Do you?"

Luke didn't like the doubting arch of Franklin's brow. "Yes, sir, I do, and I can prove it to you."

"How?" Corva asked.

Luke crossed his arms, looking as serious as he knew how. "By getting married. By letting Josephine do what she's been wanting to do for months now—send away for a bride for me, like Mrs. Piedmont did for you."

Franklin and Corva exchanged glances. Corva bit her lip, and Franklin gave her the slightest shrug. They turned back to Luke.

"Do you think you're ready for a wife?" Corva asked.

Luke instantly thought of Bonnie's place behind him. He thought of Pearl's big, round "pearls," about her rouged lips. He thought about the new houses Howard Haskell had started to construct between Paradise Ranch and town "for married couples." Most of all, he thought about the promotion he was desperate to prove he was ready for.

"Yes, ma'am, I am." He nodded, more sure than he'd ever been of anything.

Corva hummed and checked with Franklin once more. He tilted his head to the side, as if they were having a silent conversation.

"We'll see," Franklin said at last. "If you do marry, and if it agrees with you and grounds you, I might just have more responsibility I can give you."

Certain he was up to the challenge, Luke grinned from ear to ear. He reached out to shake Franklin's hand. "You won't regret it, boss, not for a minute. I'm going to go over to Josephine and Pete's place right now and ask her to send for someone tomorrow. No, tomorrow's not soon enough. Today."

He said a quick goodbye to Franklin and Corva, then rushed off down Main Street and around the corner to where Josephine and Pete lived with his two youngest siblings, Freddy and Muriel.

"What happened to you?" Muriel flinched when he burst through the kitchen door.

"Saloon fight. Is Ma home?" he rushed on, without further explanation.

Muriel gaped and sputtered, but Luke was already at the door leading to the hall and on to the front parlor when she called, "She and Mrs. Piedmont are having morning tea in the front room."

Luke marched down the hall and into the parlor, where, sure enough, Josephine and Virginia leaned toward each other over a fancy tea set, like two gossiping schoolgirls.

"Ma, I want you to find me a wife," Luke announced, planting his hands on his hips and smiling with all the confidence of a conquering hero.

Josephine and Virginia snapped straight, brows shooting to their hairlines, and turned to gape at him.

A moment later, their expressions transformed into sly smiles of triumph that were anything but surprised. The grin slipped from Luke's face, and dread pooled in his gut. Maybe he'd been a bit hasty in this decision.

"I knew you'd come around sooner or later," Josephine said. She stood and swept across the room to Luke, Virginia right behind her. "I've been hoping, and more importantly, *planning*, for this day for months."

"Yes," Virginia added as the two of them pushed him toward a flowery sofa against one wall and nudged him to sit. "Mrs. Breashears has sent us profiles of all of the young women at Hurst Home, and we've been pouring over them since then, working out exactly which girl would be right for you."

"You…have?" This might have been a good time for him to run after all. Only the promise of promotion and a better life made him stay.

"Of course, my boy," Josephine said. "I love you dearly, and I want nothing but the greatest joy for you. And as we all know, the greatest joy comes from a happy and successful marriage to a woman who suits your temperament in every—good heavens, Luke, what happened to your face?"

Josephine's expression hardened to something

midway between alarm and anger. She reached out and touched her fingertips to his swollen, purple eye.

"You're just noticing my shiner now?" Luke flinched away from her.

"You finally asked me to find you a bride. What else was I supposed to think about?" Josephine's tone turned scolding.

"Land sakes, Luke. You were in that stupid saloon fight last night, weren't you?" Virginia sighed crossed her arms. "Almost all of Howard's ranch hands and a few of mine were involved. Picked a fight with Bonneville's men, or so I hear."

"We did not pick that fight," Luke growled. "They started it with that lousy, crooked deal Bonneville worked out with Dashiell's Stockyard."

"And you decided to take it to the next level, I suppose?" Josephine pursed her lips.

"We couldn't just let them gloat like they were." It wasn't much of an excuse, and both women hummed and clucked over it.

"In light of this mess, I think I'd pick Eden Gardner over Talia Lambert," Virginia said.

Josephine leaned back, nodding at Luke and humming her assent. "Definitely Eden. Talia seems like such a sweet, sunny girl, but I think you're right about Luke needing a firmer hand after all."

"A firmer hand?" Luke scowled, leaping off the sofa to pace the room. "What's this about a firmer hand? I'm a man, Ma, not some snotty kid." He puffed up his chest and stood tall to prove the point. If only his side wasn't so sore and his left eye could open all the way.

"Come now, son, you'll like Eden Gardner." Josephine smiled and patted the spot on the sofa where Luke had been sitting. "The report Mrs. Breashears sent indicates that she's sharp, quick-witted, and tough. Apparently, she's at Hurst Home because there was some trouble with her family. Mrs. Breashears isn't specific, but it sounds like they abandoned her."

"Abandoned her?" Luke's shoulders dropped from their tight bunch. Long-dormant emotion flared from those painful days when his sour old grandfather had dumped him and his siblings at the orphanage door and walked off, two days after his parents succumbed to fever. He rubbed the back of his neck. "Is…is she pretty?"

Josephine and Virginia shared a grin. "Mrs. Breashears doesn't make judgments about the girls' appearances in her reports, but she does say that Eden has dark hair, brown eyes, and freckles."

"Freckles?" Luke's mind conjured an image of a girl of no more than fifteen bearing a face full of freckles, a shy smile, and eyes glowing with adoration. Well, he wasn't so keen on a girl that young, but the adoration and the face he could take. He nodded in consideration, then said. "All right. Sounds good. How soon can she get here?"

Josephine laughed. "In a hurry, son?"

"Yep," Luke answered before he could think better of it. He inched sideways to the tea table, searching for pastries. He hadn't eaten that morning, after all. "The cattle drive is only a month away, and Franklin will need to make a decision before that."

"Cattle drive?" Josephine asked.

"Franklin?" Virginia echoed.

Luke selected a warm muffin from a plate on the table, took a bite, and said while chewing, "I asked Franklin to let me lead the cattle drive to Culpepper. He said he needed proof that I was stable and responsible. That's why I'm here."

"Ah," the two older women said in unison.

Josephine cleared her throat, lips twitching as though she was trying not to giggle. "I'll telegraph Mrs. Breashears this afternoon to see what we can arrange."

"If she's willing, I'm certain Eden could be here by the end of the month," Virginia added. "It doesn't take that long to journey from Nashville to Haskell."

"Good." Luke stuffed the rest of the muffin in his mouth. "I'm pleased."

Josephine and Virginia tried not to laugh.

"In the meantime, you'd best clean yourself up and think about the qualities a sober and mature husband should have," Josephine said. "I'm sure Pete would be more than happy to let you know what you should expect in your new role as husband."

"I think I can manage that on my own, Ma." Luke winked and started for the door. "I'm no spring chicken."

The two older women giggled and snickered. Luke paused as he reached the door and turned to them with a scowl.

"What?" he demanded.

"Nothing, nothing." Virginia held up a hand to hide her grinning mouth.

"It's just that you may want to consider that married life is not what you're thinking it is," Josephine added.

"Ma. I'm twenty-seven years old. I've heard all about Bonnie's business," he admitted, though his cheeks flared red as he did. "I know what goes on in a marriage."

Virginia burst out in snorting chuckles.

"If you say so, my dear." Josephine's lips twitched as she gave him a downright patronizing look. "If you say so."

Chapter Two

Eden Gardner stepped down from the train, the heels of her boots clicking against the hard wooden planks of the platform, and tapped the telegram in her hand against her pursed lips. Haskell, Wyoming, her last chance for a safe, normal life. She narrowed her eyes as she glanced from the stretching, mist-shrouded mountains against the horizon, to the shimmer of heat across the summer-dried fields on one side of the town—still parched late into September—to the two- and three-story buildings lining the town's main street.

She counted what she could see from the platform—hotel, bank, mercantile, saloon, church, station house, a handful of other businesses. Not to mention the jail. Residential houses seemed to keep to the side streets, away from the main thoroughfare. Every building looked new. Fresh coats of paint, lace curtains billowing out of upstairs windows, open to combat the unseasonable heat, sanded fence rails and hitching posts between lots. Women fanned themselves as they strolled down the street, shopping baskets on their arms. Shouting children chased each other up and down the board sidewalks in front of shops. The few men she saw who weren't at work in front of their shops wore fancy clothes, stiff Stetsons, and shiny buckles. Not a one of them appeared to be armed.

Easy pickings.

She chewed her lip and shook her head, scooting to the side when a particularly rotund man who had been on the train since Cheyenne, bumped her as he disembarked. Eden clenched her jaw—and her fists—but thought better of lashing out at the man. Mama always said there was no point in picking a fight over small potatoes. Brent would have shot the man dead—and probably Mama too, while he was at it.

A shiver of fear shot town her spine. Brent was exactly why she wasn't in St. Louis anymore.

She cleared her throat and unfolded the telegram. It was an answer to one she had sent from Denver the day before, advising Mrs. Virginia Piedmont, Mr. Charlie Garrett, and Mrs. Josephine Evans—and, of course, Mr. Luke Chance—that she would be on the 10:15 from Cheyenne. It read, *"Message received. Stop. Will be there. Stop."* It didn't bother to specify *who* would be there. As long as it wasn't Brent, she'd be able to rest easy. She'd been careful about disappearing, making herself untraceable. Now she only needed to play her last card to hide herself in a new life entirely. This had to work.

Eden glanced around at what probably passed for a flurry of activity on the platform. Haskell wasn't what she would describe as a metropolis. Three passengers besides her had gotten off the train. One was a lady who was now busy hugging a slightly older woman. Probably relatives. Well-off, but not wealthy. The passenger's purse dangled from her wrist. She wasn't paying attention. Any child passing by with a sharp blade and a quick hand would eat well tonight on the contents of that purse. The other two passengers, including the man who'd bumped her, had moved on. Businessmen. Fine suits. Billfolds tucked in their jackets. Not worth the effort.

Of course, relaxed souls without a care in the world were a sign of peace and prosperity. Lord knew she could use some of that. The prospect of picking up her life and moving it to a place she'd never been, barely heard of, to marry a man sight unseen was a daunting one, but it was still better than the constant suspicion and frazzled nerves that her life back East had descended into. A little peace and quiet would be a godsend. Marriage, homemaking, popping out a couple babies—Eden was ready for it all.

The focal point of the action on the platform centered around a tired-looking man in his thirties—the stationmaster, judging by the uniform—and two porters who helped him unload the train, one of whom couldn't have been more than fifteen. The stationhouse door had been left open, a desk was visible from where Eden stood. She grunted in disgust and shook her head. It would take her less than a minute to waltz into the stationhouse, find the cashbox, and walk out, and no one would be the wiser. She'd probably even have time to pick the cashbox's lock. Easy as pie. If that was the life she was still after.

Not anymore.

Shaking her head, she marched to the side, approaching the younger porter. She reached into the buttoned pocket inside of her traveling jacket that held her reticule, taking out her luggage ticket and tucking away the telegram.

"Excuse me." She tapped the young porter's shoulder. "Here's my ticket."

The young man—who had the same coloring as the

stationmaster, probably his son—straightened and gawped at her.

"My luggage ticket?" She held out the ticket with a reassuring smile. No sense in giving the poor boy any reason to be suspicious of her.

"Oh. Oh, right. Sorry. I'm kinda new to the job, but Pa needed help and…" He cleared his throat. "Your luggage. Right. Sorry."

He took her ticket with a bashful smile, scrambling off to the open doors of the luggage car. He was sweet, really, all bright eyes and eagerness. And helping his father. Eden always approved of that. Sleepy old Haskell had its charms beyond being in the middle of nowhere.

"Miss Eden Gardner?"

Eden spun as her name was called. Right away, she spotted a distinguished gentlemen in an expensive suit, a gold watch fob glistening across his waistcoat, and an attractive older woman in sensible but stylish cotton.

"Miss Eden Gardner," the woman said, a statement this time instead of a question. She picked up her pace, coming forward with outstretched hands. "I'm Mrs. Josephine Evans, and you have no idea how overjoyed I am to welcome you to Haskell."

"She took the words right out of my mouth," the gentleman said. He came to a stop in front of her and touched the brim of his hat before taking her hand in a firm shake. "Charlie Garrett, at your service."

"It's a pleasure to meet both of you." She wasn't even lying at that. Her shoulders relaxed and her back stopped aching. It was because of these two, and Mrs. Piedmont, that she was getting this one-in-a-million chance to start over.

As soon as she let go of Mr. Garrett's hand, she

searched behind him, scanning the area around the station. "Where's my husband?"

Mrs. Evans's brow shot up. Mr. Garrett sputtered, then burst into a hearty laugh. "No beating around the bush with you, I guess."

Eden crossed her arms and smiled at him. Handsome, tail end of his prime. Confident, competent, and likely able to take her down before she knew what was happening. Yes, she liked Charlie Garrett at first sight.

"I never saw much point in beating around any bushes," she told him and Mrs. Evans. "It's a waste of time when seconds matter."

"Is that so?" Mr. Garrett's lips twitched as he worked to get his grin under control. His eyes held experience, understanding, knowing. She'd have to watch out for him.

A slow but equally satisfied grin spread across Mrs. Evans's face. "Oh yes," she said, rubbing her hands together as though relishing a prize. "She'll be perfect. Luke won't know what hit him."

Damn. By the sound of things, Eden would get along with Mrs. Evans like they were two peas in a pod. And if what Mrs. Breashears had said was right, Mrs. Evans was Luke Chance's adopted mother, which meant she'd be Eden's mother-in-law. Haskell was growing on her already.

"I'm here, I'm here!" a call came from the row of hitching posts to one side of the train. "Sorry I'm late."

Mr. Garrett and Mrs. Evans turned, and Eden leaned to the side, arms still crossed, to get a look at the man who was climbing down from a handsome chestnut gelding. He moved with the horse as though the two of them had one mind, looping the reins around the post with hardly a glance. When he turned in Eden's direction, her heart stuttered in her chest.

"Well, *hello*," she hummed.

The man strode forward with wide, sure steps. Cocky steps. The kind of steps that said he could handle any situation and keep smiling while doing so. His shoulders were broad, his arms strong under sleeves rolled up past his elbow. A hint of dark blond hair was visible under the brim of his worn hat, and straight, white teeth flashed as he smiled. He hopped up onto the platform with ease. Eden had half a mind to ask him to turn around so she could get a look at his backside.

"Are you Eden Gardner?" he asked, striding to a stop between Mr. Garrett and Mrs. Evans. He raked her from head to toe with a fiery gaze that said he liked what he saw.

Hot damn.

"That's me." She stepped toward him, holding out a hand.

He took it, his grip firm and warm. "Luke Chance. Pleased to meet you."

His confidence, his strength, that hint of mischief in his eyes as he smiled at her—yep, she could have done much worse in a man. Now all she needed to do was make sure he sealed the deal before he saw right through her and called it all off.

"All right." She looked at Mr. Garrett, then Mrs. Evans. "He seems like he's got all the right parts in all the right places. I'll marry him." She nodded. The faster the better.

Mr. Garrett swallowed another snort of laughter. Mrs. Evans looked like she might crow.

Luke Chance's grin faltered, and he darted a look between Mrs. Evans and Mr. Garrett, then narrowed his eyes at Eden. "Didn't you already agree to marry me when you got on that train?"

Eden shrugged. "Figured it'd be best if I got a look at you before truly making up my mind." She feigned confidence to hide her desperation, even from herself, and raked him with the same assessing look that he'd given her. "You look good. Pretty face, strong arms. I can live with that." She pivoted to the train, frowning. "Where did that porter get off to with my trunk?"

"I'll handle it," Luke said, jumping into action. He still looked a fair bit baffled, but he marched off across the platform to the open door of the train's luggage car without a lick of hesitation. "Hey, Athos, I'm here to fetch Miss Eden Gardner's luggage," he told the stationmaster with just the right amount of authority in his voice.

A grin played across Eden's lips as he leaned into the luggage car, his trousers pulling tight against his rump. Nothing to be ashamed of there. He knew how to take charge of a situation too, by the look of things. It'd be easy as pie to entrust her safety to a man who knew how to get things done. And she knew a trick or two about how to make him want her. This plan was going to work after all.

"I think Mr. Luke Chance and I are going to get along just fine," she hummed, settling back on her heels to watch him. Her soon-to-be-husband was quite a sight.

"Come on now, Hubert," Luke called down the length of the luggage car to where Athos's boy was yanking a long, narrow trunk free from a pile of others. "It's not like that's a full steamer trunk. Your last name isn't Strong for nothing. Give it a push."

Hubert grunted. "I've just about got it."

Luke nodded, then glanced over his shoulder to see if Eden Gardner was watching. A sizzle shot down his spine—lighting up a few precious things below his belt that shouldn't have been lit in public—when he saw that she was. His mail-order bride wasn't just watching him, she was *perusing* him. Her pert, cupid's-bow of a mouth ticked to the side in an appreciative grin. Her dark eyes flashed with curiosity. Hell, he'd never had a girl look at him like that before, at least not outside of the saloon. But Bonnie's girls batted their eyelashes more at the cash he carried and the hope that he might put it to good use, for a change, than at him. Good girls definitely weren't supposed to give fellows they'd just met the eye like that.

Lord above, what if Eden was at Hurst Home because she'd been working at a place like Bonnie's? Would he mind if his wife had that sort of a past? Another warm shiver passed down his spine, making parts of him jumpier than fire in a windstorm, at the prospect. Hell no, he wouldn't mind.

"Here you go, Luke." Hubert groaned as he carried the long trunk enclosed by iron bands and a huge lock to the door. "Careful, it's heavy."

"I think I can manage," he told the boy with a wry grin. But when Hubert squatted to hand the trunk over, Luke sagged under its weight. "What does she have in here?"

"Lead pipes?" Hubert suggested, hopping down from the car.

It sure felt like it. Luke adjusted his grip on the trunk's handles, bracing it to the point where the muscles of his arms strained against his shirt. He pasted on a smile as he turned to Eden, Josephine, and Charlie. He wasn't about to make a fool of himself by looking like the trunk was heavy.

Fighting the sheen of sweat breaking out on his back, he strode over to Eden and grinned. "Where do you want it?"

Eden's lips twitched, one dark eyebrow flickered up. She bit her lip, and said with a saucy hum, "Anywhere you want to put it, sweetie."

Luke nearly dropped the dang trunk on his foot. With the state her look and that comment had him in, it likely would have hit something precious on the way down. The sweat dripping down his back doubled, and not because of the weight in his arms.

Josephine seemed to find the situation too funny to say anything. She had turned half away, her hand covering her mouth, as she pinched her lips shut to keep from saying anything. Typical Ma. Charlie was the one who answered, "I'm sure Herb Waters has a wagon you can rent for the afternoon, unless you can find someone heading out to Paradise Ranch who'd be willing to transport the trunk." He shifted, spotting something in the street. "There you go, there's Cody Montrose. He can take care of it for you."

Arms aching with the strain of holding the trunk, Luke glanced over his shoulder. Cody was walking at a leisurely pace from Cyrus Avenue toward the saddle-maker's. Luke filled his lungs to call to his friend.

"What do you need him for?" Eden cut him off. Luke whipped to face her. "Luke is perfectly capable of handling things himself, aren't you, sweetie?"

Her words had more of the ring of a statement of fact than a question about his competence. It was nice of her to build him up like that without knowing him…but why was she? A new, more deep-set tingle joined the one centered in his groin.

"Yeah, of course I can handle it," he told her, nodding to Charlie for good measure. He hefted the trunk higher in his arms and started for the edge of the platform. "Come on, Eden. We'll drop this off at Waters' Livery, get Herb to ready a wagon for us, then we'll pop over to the church and get hitched."

"Fine by me," Eden answered with a broad grin.

"I'll just pick up the flowers Theophilus Gunn has arranged for your bouquet at the hotel, and I'll meet you at the church," Josephine said.

"You're coming to the wedding?" Eden's smile brightened.

"Honey, I wouldn't miss this for the world." Josephine gave Eden a wink.

It occurred to Luke as he and Eden started down the road that he might want to second guess anything his ma said in that tone of voice, but right at that moment, he was too pleased with himself for carrying a heavy trunk and making it look easy, and for taking charge of his almost-wife's welfare.

"The livery is just down here." He motioned to the left with his head when they stepped onto the dust of Main Street.

"Lead on," Eden said with a satisfied grin.

Luke was inclined to go above and beyond to make sure she stayed satisfied in every way. If he'd known getting married would be this sweet, he would have done it a long time ago.

Ahead of them, Cody slowed his steps, waiting for Luke and Eden to catch up. "What's all this? You suddenly decide work is a good idea?"

The sweat down Luke's back turned cold, and a frown creased his forehead. He shot a sideways glance to Eden to see what she thought of Cody's teasing. The only change to her expression was mild curiosity.

"You know me, Cody. I always work hard." He widened his eyes, tilting his head to Eden, hoping she didn't notice and that Cody got the point.

He was out of luck. Cody snorted. "I *do* know you, and hard work isn't in your dictionary. Well, not unless whiskey or women are involved." He winked at Eden.

Cody was a friend, but if Luke wasn't holding a heavy trunk in his arms, he would have knocked a few of his teeth out. He had to settle for a dark scowl.

Eden crossed her arms and rested her weight on one hip. "And who, might I ask, are you?"

Cody puffed up his chest, grinned like a cat, and said, "Cody Montrose, ma'am. You must be new around here, otherwise I would have snatched you up long ago."

Yep, Luke was definitely going to take Cody out in back of the sheds later and teach him some manners. They reached the yard outside of Waters' Livery, and Luke deposited Eden's trunk in Herb's wagon-for-rent beside the fence, then turned to give Cody a piece of his mind.

Oddly enough, Eden laughed at Cody's outrageous flirting. "You'll have to fight your way through my fiancé if you want to make eyes at me like that, Cody Montrose."

"You've got a fiancé?"

"For about ten more minutes." Eden nodded to Luke. "Come on, sweetie. We've got an appointment at the church."

"Why all the hurry?" Cody asked, spreading his arms.

"No hurry," Eden was quick to reply. "Come on." She tugged on Luke's arm.

Luke shot Cody a self-satisfied smile, then nodded to Herb as the older man sauntered out of the livery's office. "Hey Herb, mind if I borrow the wagon for the afternoon? I've got a trunk to drive back to the ranch."

"Not a problem," Herb said. "It isn't reserved until Thursday. It'll be fifty cents, provided you get it back before sundown."

"Sure thing. But I've got one errand to run first."

"Errand?" Herb peeked at Eden.

"Getting married," Eden answered. "To me. Right now."

Herb gaped, then burst into laughter. Eden winked at him, then stepped around the wagon and back into the street. Luke flashed a triumphant grin at Herb, then started after her.

"Wait, no! I get it now." Cody caught up to them. "You're Eden Gardner? Wasn't that the name of the bride you sent away for, Luke?"

"Yep," Eden clipped without stopping. "That's me."

"That's her," Luke added with a grin as wide as the horizon. Married life just kept getting better and better, and he wasn't actually married yet. Any woman that could set Cody down when he got impertinent was his kind of woman.

Cody snorted in disbelief and matched his stride to Luke's. "But she's not at all like Franklin's wife."

"Who, Corva Collier?" Eden asked, still walking at a fast clip.

Luke's brow shot up. "You know Corva?"

"Of course I do." Eden grinned and touched his arm. "She had the room across the hall from mine at Hurst Home from last fall up until she came out here in the spring. Corva's a darling. Sweetest girl you'll ever meet and a good friend."

"Then how come she never said anything about you?" Luke asked.

Eden glanced at him as they turned off the road that ran parallel to the railroad tracks and on to a path that stretched across a wide field to a quaint, whitewashed church with stained-glass windows. A flash of suspicion darkened her eyes. "Did you ask her about me?"

A sheepish flush filled Luke's cheeks. "Well, no, not exactly."

Eden shrugged, loosening in relief. "I'm sure she would have told you everything you'd wanted to know." She tossed him a flirty smile, then hurried up the church steps to the door.

Luke watched the bounce of her step, the swish of the mass of chocolate-brown hair that swung free down her back in tempting waves, the curve of her hips in her simple traveling dress. Curves like those were dangerous. Hell, a smile like hers could cause a man to do some dangerous things. So why in creation was she in such a hurry to marry *him*?

Cody stepped up beside him and slapped a hand on his shoulder. "That settles it. Sweet Corva and spicy Eden. I'm asking Mrs. Piedmont, Mrs. Evans, and Mr. Garrett to get me a wife too."

"Do what you like." Luke nudged his friend. "This one's mine."

He climbed the church steps two at a time, eager to march down the aisle.

Chapter Three

By the time he was standing at the front of the church, Eden's arm looped through his, Cody standing in on the spur of the moment as his best man, and Josephine witnessing from Eden's other side, it dawned on Luke that he didn't know much about weddings. They'd always been annoyances to him—long, boring ceremonies that no one was interested in except the women. He knew that he was supposed to say "I do" when asked, and that the bride pledged to love, honor, and obey the groom, but the whole bit about forsaking all others? Well, he guessed he could manage that.

"Then by the power invested in me by God and the Territory of Wyoming, I now pronounce you husband and wife," Rev. Pickering said with a smile. "You may kiss your bride."

A funny little shiver zipped down Luke's spine as he pivoted to face Eden. That was it? That's all it took to get married? He tried to smile at…at his *wife*, but his lips seemed to have forgotten how to manage it. They wobbled around—just like his heart—restless with the suspicion that he might just have taken on more than he could chew.

Things like responsibility and leadership looked a whole lot easier when you didn't have to worry about them, but now he was a husband. It was his job to protect this firecracker of a woman…a woman who he barely knew. What the hell had he gotten himself into?

To top it all off, Eden looked more relieved than anything else. Her cheeks were positively pink with it. Had she thought he would back down after making her travel half the country to be his bride?

Whatever she thought, she arched a brow. "You planning on kissing me any time soon or are you still thinking about it?"

Her saucy stance shook Luke out of whatever that was holding him back. He brushed those worried thoughts aside and slipped his arms around Eden's waist, tugging her close. She gasped in surprise, and a surge of heat rushed through him.

"I'm definitely planning on kissing you, Mrs. Chance."

"Oh!"

Before Eden could finish the quick, excited syllable, or hand off her wedding bouquet to Josephine, Luke swooped down and captured her mouth in a kiss that could give old ladies apoplexy. Kissing his wife was as easy as falling off a log. Eden had lush, full lips and warm skin that smelled like brown sugar in the sun. She was no fainting daisy either. She dropped her bouquet and tossed her arms over his shoulders with a low hum, her lips parting to both accept and tease his. She traced her tongue along Luke's, causing a shudder that landed square in his groin. He lowered a hand to Eden's backside and nudged her closer before remembering that his ma was standing four feet away, and they were in church.

He broke the kiss with a sharp intake of breath and

settled Eden back on her feet. "I think I'm gonna like this whole being married thing," he said, sounding like a wolf who was ready to devour a sheep.

"I can think of worse things to do with my time," Eden answered, sliding her hands down his arms. She had fire in her eyes now that the two of them were a done deal, that was for sure.

A tickle at the back of Luke's mind wondered where such a sweet-faced young woman would gain that kind of experience, but an even bigger part of him didn't give a lick.

"That's it." Cody stepped forward to slap Luke's back. "Mrs. Evans, I want you to find me a girl like Eden here to marry."

Josephine met the comment with a wry laugh. "We'll see, Cody." She shook her head and rested a hand on Eden's shoulder. "You two all set?"

"Yes, ma'am, I believe we are," Eden answered.

"Good. Because I've got a meeting with Olivia Garrett about refurbishing some of the schoolrooms, and I'm already late."

"You go on, Ma." Luke stepped toward her and planted a grateful kiss on her cheek. "You're leaving me in good hands."

"Oh, I know I am." Josephine exchanged a mischievous glance with Eden before turning and marching up the aisle and out of the church.

"See you back at the ranch." Cody gave Luke's back one last thump, nodded to Eden, then turned and strode up the aisle after Josephine, chuckling all the way.

"I've just got a few papers for you to sign that I need to file with Howard and the territory, then you're good to go," Rev. Pickering said.

The official business of getting married took about

five minutes. After that, Luke escorted his beautiful new bride out of the church and into the sunshine of Haskell in late summer.

"What a beautiful day, don't you think, Mrs. Chance?" Luke drawled as he strolled down the path toward the road.

"Finest I've had in a long time," Eden answered, then sighed happily. "If I forget to say it later, I really am grateful to you for going through with this."

Luke flinched to stare at her. "Why wouldn't I go through with it? I need you."

Eden's brow flew up in disbelief, then she laughed. "Well, that's a first. I can't say that I've ever been needed by a man before."

"Then you've just been around the wrong men."

"Tell me about it," she drawled.

Luke narrowed his eyes as he steered her in the opposite direction from the livery, up to the baseball field, and around back of the town so he could show Eden her new hometown. "Maybe you should tell me about them?" he suggested.

Eden snorted, her face pinching into a scowl. "Not much to tell. I have brothers, that's all." A dark flush came to her cheeks that could have been embarrassment or anger. Either way, it was fetching.

"I have a brother and two sisters," Luke shared. "My older sister, Libby, married a man in Oregon and lives up there on a timber operation with him and their two kids. My little brother, Freddy, is a right menace these days now that he thinks he's grown up, but my sister, Muriel, is a sweetheart."

"I look forward to meeting them." Eden nodded.

She glanced around, taking in the sights that Luke walked her past. Her gaze went up to the tops of the buildings, her eyes narrowing in concentration, maybe even calculation. Luke might not have known much about his wife yet, but the way she looked at things told him she was smart as a tack. She didn't just look, she *figured*. Right now, she appeared to be figuring how the buildings of Haskell were constructed. Or maybe how they were situated. It was hard to tell.

"Why did they build the bank next to the mercantile?" she asked, nodding to the two buildings as they rounded the corner at the top of Main Street, the opposite side from the railroad tracks.

Luke shrugged. "I suppose Howard figured folks would want to go shopping straight off as soon as they picked up their money from the bank."

Eden hummed. "Not very smart. One man could rob the bank and another the mercantile at the same time, and if they had their horses waiting between the two, they could get away before anyone had a chance to sound the alarm." She twisted to study the street further, then said, "Yep, with the jail all the way down the street near the train station, bandits could make off with a wad of cash before the sheriff could catch up to them." She glanced sideways at Luke. "Haskell does have a sheriff, doesn't it?"

The hair on the back of Luke's neck stood up for some reason. Did he say his wife was smart? Diabolical was more like it.

Hell, he was the luckiest man alive.

"Trey Knighton." He nodded, grinning from ear to ear. "He's the sheriff. You're not planning on robbing any banks, are you?"

"No." She brushed the idea off as though it were ridiculous. "I haven't robbed a bank in years."

He laughed, loving his new wife's sense of humor. Because she was joking, of course. Right?

"Who's that?" She nodded over to the bank where a tall, distinguished-looking black man in a suit that would make the finest tailors in San Francisco jealous was busy talking to a middle-aged man with snow-shite hair.

"Which one?" Luke asked. "The dandy is Solomon Templesmith, Haskell's banker and richest man, other than Howard Haskell and Rex Bonneville."

"He's black," Eden observed.

"You've got a good eye," Luke drawled. "He's also brilliant, savvy, and ruthless when it comes to money. The man talking to him is Theophilus Gunn, the manager of the Cattleman Hotel. If you ever need anything done, no matter how complex or complicated, ask Gunn. He's one in a million."

Eden hummed, and her eyes moved on. "Don't you have a hairdresser? A dress shop?"

Luke blinked and rubbed the back of his neck. "Why would we need them? Don't ladies like to sew their own dresses and brush their own hair?"

Eden snorted and shook her head. "This town was founded by men, wasn't it?"

"What makes you say that?"

Eden raised a hand to point. "Bank, mercantile, saloon, jail, and *that.*" She ended by pointing straight at Bonnie's place—where several of the girls had draped themselves on the porch wearing little more than skivvies, and were fanning themselves in the heat.

Luke stopped, lips twitching. "Say, you didn't, by any chance, used to work at a place like that, did you?"

"No," Eden giggled, amused instead of offended, thank heavens.

"Oh.   Good."   Luke   shrugged.   "I   just

thought...because you didn't mind kissing a man you barely met and all...and because of that thing you said back at the station."

She dropped his arm and planted a fist on his hips. "So are you saying a woman has to be either a blushing miss or a whore? That she can't kiss her husband like she means it without having low morals, or appreciate the sight of a finely formed rump?"

"Um...well...I..." Oh Lord, he was in trouble now, and he hadn't even been married an hour.

Eden burst into a laugh as he squirmed. She punched his arm, then looped her hand through it. "Don't worry. I know how things go. I have brothers, remember? And no sisters. Plus, Ma died after..." She cleared her throat, but didn't elaborate.

Luke breathed in relief. "Oh. Okay, I see." That didn't mean he didn't feel like she'd knocked his heart down to his boots and back.

"But women do like *those things* too, you know," she added, almost as if she was telling him a secret.

"Of course they do," Luke said, although his thoughts ran more along the lines of "They do?"

As they passed in front of Bonnie's, the woman herself stepped out onto the porch, Rex Bonneville right behind her.

"Girls, what are you doing?" Bonnie said, crossing her arms and tapping one white-leather-booted foot. Bonnie was an imposing woman who held herself with authority and never had a hair out of place. She was surprisingly young too—not even thirty. Why she had established a whorehouse in Haskell instead of marrying was almost as much of a mystery as why she spent time with Rex Bonneville.

The girls on the porch rushed to sit straight, adjusting

their scant clothing to be as modest as possible, which was a feat. Eden shifted her weight to one hip and watched the unfolding scene, a smirk tilting her lips. As soon as he was certain she wouldn't expire with shock and indignation, Luke relaxed and observed as well.

"It's just that it's so hot out here, Miss Bonnie," Pearl sighed, giving herself another fan. "It doesn't feel like September at all."

"Yeah," caramel-skinned Domenica agreed. "Couldn't we do our entertaining down at the swimming hole until the weather gets more like it's supposed to this time of year?"

Luke started to chuckle, but his amusement was cut off by the deadly glance Bonneville shot at him. Bonneville took a few solid strides to the end of the porch, tucking his thumbs in the pockets of his vest and pulling himself up to his full, impressive height.

"What are you gloating at, boy?" he growled.

The need to stand up to the likes of Bonneville and show what kind of man he was warred with concern over what Eden would think. Luke glanced sideways at his wife, then stood straighter and answered, "Nothing. Just giving my lady wife a tour of her new hometown."

Bonneville split into a cold smile. "What woman in her right mind would marry one of Howard Haskell's flunkies?"

The same, boiling rage that had come over Luke the night of the saloon fight bubbled up again. Who the hell did Bonneville think he was to push people around and talk down to them like he was better than everybody?

"This is Eden," he said, jaw stiff. "And a finer woman you'll never meet. So I'd appreciate it if you'd show some manners, sir."

Bonneville's face splotched red. "I won't have common toughs talking to me like that."

"Then you'd better pack up and move someplace else." Luke stood his ground.

Bonneville's cold gaze snapped to Eden. "You know your new husband was in jail less than a month ago?"

Icy prickles worked their way down Luke's arms and legs. He'd hoped there would be time to explain that saloon fight and what caused it before Eden found out.

"Really?" Eden tugged at Luke's arm, her hand still resting in the crook of his elbow. "Well, good for you."

Luke's brow shot up—it might as well just stay there, seeing how much it was heading there that day—at the sly grin Eden wore.

She squared her shoulders and nodded, chin first, at Bonneville. "Who are you?"

Judging by the dark anger in Bonneville's eyes, he didn't like the sharp question. "I'm Rex Bonneville, and if you don't wipe that smug little grin off your shrewish face, I'll—"

"Rex." Bonnie stepped forward, placing a calming hand on Bonneville's arm. She looked him in the eye, hard as iron. Rex clamped his mouth shut, and Bonnie turned to Luke and Eden. "It's a pleasure to meet you, Mrs. Chance. I heard you were coming."

"Did you?" Eden brightened.

Bonnie glanced to Luke. "Well, I heard Luke had sent away for a girl from Hurst Home, like Franklin Haskell did. I think it's rather noble of Mr. Garrett to set girls up that way." She lowered her voice and added, "So they don't end up working for me."

For a moment, Luke had that tricky feeling that Bonnie might be the most unhappy person in Haskell, in spite of her fancy clothes and boots and the income from her girls.

"Come along, Rex," she sighed, tugging Bonneville's arm and starting into the street with him. "Mr. Dashiell is waiting for us."

Bonneville sniffed at Luke, then walked on with Bonnie as if Luke didn't exist. Luke would have ignored him too, but for Bonnie's last statement.

"That snake will get what's coming to him one day," he muttered.

"What'd he do?" Eden asked, pulling him along the street on their way to the livery.

"Dashiell," Luke said. "He's the other snake, the one that owns the nearest stockyard to here. Bonneville somehow got him in his pocket. The two of them signed an exclusive agreement for the use of the stockyard and rail services."

"What does that mean?"

"It means we have to drive our cattle an extra hundred or so miles to get to another stockyard where they can be loaded onto the train."

Eden hummed. "Isn't that a terrible deal on this Dashiell's part? He'll be losing business."

"Bonneville fixed him up somehow, the slimy bastard." He winced at his cursing.

"Schemers rarely end up getting what they think they're gonna get, and usually end up with what they deserve," Eden said, ignoring his loose language.

Luke's mouth twitched into a smile. "I like the sound of that."

She grinned at him, squeezing his arm. "Then we're gonna get along just fine."

*   *   *

Eden knew she shouldn't be giggling as she rode on the wagon bench beside Luke. They were passing through beautiful, expansive fields dotted with late-summer wildflowers, a stream flowing to one side. She should appreciate nature. She always had liked riding through open land with her brothers, even if they were laying low or scouting out new targets. But the pure joy of knowing she'd gambled her life and won in spectacular fashion had her bubbling over. *This* was the kind of place she could stay hidden. *This* was where she could breathe at last. As long as she kept a smile on Luke's face.

"Is something funny?" Luke shot her a sideways look, his mouth tight. "Something I said?"

He tugged on the lines to steer the horse pulling the wagon off of the main road and on toward a cluster of buildings in various stages of construction.

"No." Eden laughed outright. "I'm just too pleased with how everything has turned out so far to hold it all inside, you know?" She faced him, raising her hand to shield her eyes from the sun.

Luke warmed to a smile. "I sure am pleased you're pleased." He nodded, then tilted his head to the side, then winced. "I just wish Bonneville hadn't soured my mood with his ugly face back at Bonnie's."

"Why should you let the likes of him bother you?"

Luke barked a low laugh. "If you're gonna live in Haskell, then you'll know all the reasons why soon enough."

"How about knowing them now?" She planted her hands on the edge of the bench and leaned toward him.

"All right. Here's the way things are in Haskell. Howard Haskell, my boss, founded the town about ten years ago. He's a wealthy rancher, but rather than spending his money on fancy clothes and trips and things, he built a town. Then Bonneville came along, bought up the land next to Paradise Ranch and went into business for himself."

"So?" Eden shrugged. "The open range is huge, or so I hear tell. There's room and business enough for everyone."

"Yeah, but the open range is closing as ranchers fence their patches in with that new barbed wire stuff. And Bonneville's not the kind of man who likes competition. Howard may own the town, but Bonneville joined the Wyoming Stock Grower's Association. He's got power and Howard's got power, and they're always thinking of ways to cut each other down and take the whole prize."

He pulled the wagon to a stop at the entrance to a circular drive with five half-built houses, complete with outbuildings and yards, around them. Half a dozen men climbed over one of the houses, accompanied by the sounds of nails being hammered and boards being sawed. The air smelled of sawdust and hard work.

Eden snorted. "Well, if that's not men for you, I don't know what is. Always trying to be king of the hill, even when there's plenty of hill to go around."

Luke shot her a doubtful look before hopping down and striding around to her side of the wagon. Before he got there to help her, Eden climbed down herself.

"There's nothing wrong with a man wanting to take charge of what's his, especially if he's got plans of how he wants to run things," Luke said.

Eden brushed her skirts straight then turned to face him. "Is that you?" she asked. "Do you want to take charge of what's yours and run it?"

A strong "yes" look came over him—squared shoulders, set jaw, determination in his eyes. An excited shiver swirled through Eden's gut. Two seconds later, that mighty look melted to uncertainty.

"I guess." Luke shrugged, scratching his chin. "That is, if you don't mind."

Eden laughed, reaching up to pat his cheek. "Sweetie, as long as you keep me safe and warm at night with a steady supply of food on my table and a handful of babies to chase around, I'll be happy as a hog in a bog."

She pivoted to look at the houses under construction, considering the issue settled. Luke, on the other hand, kicked a toe in the dirt of the drive, watching her.

"That's really what you want?" he asked. "A house, kids, normal, boring stuff?"

She planted a hand on her hip and stared at him. "I haven't had a normal day in my life. Boring is a dream come true for me. Now, what are these houses?"

She faced the houses, studying the construction once more. Two stories, sizeable, room for a garden behind.

"Huh." Luke took a step forward, gesturing for her to come with him. "I never thought boring would be someone's dream." He paused, the sound of their steps crunching across rocky ground filling the silence, then said, "Hurst Home is a place where women can go when they're in danger, right?"

Ah. So there were brains in her sweet husband's head after all. "Yep," she answered aloud. "And you better believe that half or more of the girls there are beside themselves with eagerness to come out here to pokey, quiet, old Haskell to get away from it."

A grin tweaked the corner of Luke's mouth. "You escaping danger?"

She returned his grin with a sly smile. "I just want a normal life."

Luke stepped closer to her, coming to a stop in front

of one of the houses and sliding his arm around her waist. Eden's heart twanged in her chest. She cleared her throat and brushed the unusual reaction aside. She liked the feel of Luke's arm around her, that was all. Her heart had nothing to do with it.

"What we've got here is one of Howard's brilliant ideas," Luke explained. "It's called The Village. Charlie Garrett, Mrs. Piedmont, and my ma may have come up with the idea of bringing ladies out here from Hurst Home, but Howard was the one who decided to throw in the incentive that any man who accepts a wife from the home will be given a house and property of his own."

Eden nearly choked in surprise. "Mr. Haskell is giving away houses?"

"Yes he is." Luke nodded, then shrugged. "Well, technically they're on loan until you pay them off, but he's giving us remarkable terms on the mortgage and a lot of guarantees for the future."

Eden whistled her disbelief and appreciation. "So which one is ours?"

"This one, I expect." Luke nodded to the nearest house, the one that was closest to completion. "Want to take a look?"

"Absolutely."

She broke away from him and strode ahead. The house that would be theirs looked close to being completed, at least from the outside. Already, she could see herself rocking a baby on the shaded front porch, waving to neighbors across the circle, and planting flowers along the front drive. The door was open, so she walked right in, breathing in the scent of fresh wood and promise.

One quick walk through the downstairs showed her that there was no stove or sink in the kitchen yet, but there were places for them. The walls were bare wood without plaster or paint, but the fireplace in the front room was finished, and glass windows had been installed throughout. There was even a fancy, modern indoor water closet, although she'd spotted an outhouse in the back through one of the windows.

"You like it?" Luke asked when she finally stopped moving and simply stood in the spacious dining room.

Eden let out a sigh. "It's perfect."

Perfect and protected and as far away from the chaos and uncertainty of life with her brothers. They would never guess where she'd gone, never dream of her settling in a place like this, and as far as she was concerned, that was the best feature of all. If they didn't imagine her becoming a simple rancher's wife out West, then they wouldn't get it in their heads to look for her.

"Right." She twisted to face Luke, hands on her hips. "So clearly we're not shacking up here tonight. Where do we hang our boots until the house is ready?"

A whimsical grin flickered across Luke's features. "Howard thought of that too. Come on, I'll show you."

He reached for her hand, and Eden was more than happy to take it. It wasn't just the house or the peaceful, frontier town. It was the handsome, motivated husband she'd landed herself that made this such a good deal. Lord, she couldn't wait to get him wherever it was they were going and peel his clothes off to see what he was made of.

"This Village is halfway between town and Paradise Ranch," Luke explained once they were on the road again. "But for now, most of Howard's employees—Mrs. Piedmont's employees too, since she owns half the ranch—live in bunk-houses. Howard decided that newlyweds need a little privacy until their houses are done. So he built the Hen House."

Eden snorted with laughter. "Hen House?"

Luke shook his head, chuckling. "I wasn't the one who named it, trust me."

They drove on, through parched landscape and under a sweeping arch with the words "Paradise Ranch" worked in iron filigree. Before they had gone more than a hundred yards, Eden saw the herd and gasped.

"I don't think I've ever seen so many cows in one place in my life," she said, pressing a hand to her chest.

"They're usually more spread out, scattered all across the range. But the drive starts tomorrow, so we've corralled them into this area," Luke explained.

"There must be hundreds of them." The wild urge to count every head welled up in Eden, but she didn't know where to start. "How long does it take to drive them?"

Luke shrugged. "This is the first time we have to take them all the way to the Culpepper stockyard, so we're not exactly sure. A couple weeks?"

Eden hummed. She's spent weeks on end living rough off the land more than a couple of times, but not with hundreds of cattle to watch out for.

Those thoughts were cut short as Luke nudged her and pointed on to a cluster of buildings—including a large, fine house—ahead of them.

"There you go." He nodded. "Howard's bit of the ranch and all his buildings, including that whitewashed one, the Hen House. We're home."

Chapter Four

Howard Haskell knew exactly what he was doing when he built the Hen House. Although Luke suspected that Mrs. Elizabeth Haskell was the one who spearheaded the design. Eden's eyes lit up when Luke escorted her up the shallow steps to the small front porch, then on inside into the main room.

The Hen House had three main rooms—a central room with a sofa and chairs, dining room table, and cabinet, a bedroom with a single, large bed and a bureau, and a fully-stocked kitchen. It was snug and cozy, but it wasn't designed to be lived in for a long period of time. There wasn't much space, but that didn't seem to bother Eden at all.

"It's lovely," she sighed, turning a circle in the main room. "A bride could feel right at home here."

"I think that's the point." Luke tried to keep the grunt out of his voice as he carried her trunk inside. "Where do you want this?"

Eden finished her circle by facing him, her pretty face sporting a blush that made Luke want to drop the trunk where they were and kiss her. She scanned the room, skipped over to the open bedroom door, and peeked inside.

"In here."

Luke followed her, turning sideways to squeeze through the bedroom door with the trunk. A rush of heat struck him at the sight of the big bed. Now there was something he was looking forward to. But not with a trunk in his arms.

"Put it on the bed for now," Eden instructed him, her lips twitching with amusement when she saw where his gaze had landed.

Luke's heated thoughts cooled. "The bed? You sure?"

"Yes." She rested one hand on her hip, gesturing to the bed with the other.

"You, uh, sure you don't want me to put it somewhere else so we can test out the bed first?" He winked at her for good measure.

The way Eden's grin grew to something akin to a furnace had Luke itching to put the trunk down and get on with things. "In a hurry there, sweetie?"

"Yes, ma'am," he teased her right back. And why not? She was his wife, she'd been giving him the eye since she got off the train, and it was about damn time she made a man of him.

She took a few steps toward him that caused her hips to sway. Luke barely knew which curves to ogle.

"Sweetie, I've been on a train for the last four days. I haven't eaten since breakfast. Sure, I could use a little roll in the hay to limber up my stiff muscles, but I kinda want to unpack and eat supper first. But later…" She twisted away, still looking at him over her shoulder, and nodded to the bed. "Put the trunk on the bed."

Luke's jaw went slack. Well, didn't that just beat all?

He was in serious trouble. Then again, he never did mind a little trouble now and then.

Stifling a chuckle and warning himself to keep his hands to himself for now to reap the benefits later, he set the heavy trunk on the bed. His muscles ached with relief as he let go, and the bed sagged.

"What've you got in there that weighs so much, darling?" He tested out the endearment, trying to decide if it suited her.

"Nothing you need to worry your pretty little head about."

His temptation to ask what that meant was blown away as she grabbed two handfuls of his shirt, lifted to her toes, and kissed him. All thought ceased as their lips met and mingled. Need deeper than anything he'd ever felt gripped him, igniting him body and soul. The pressure of his pants getting tighter only fueled the fire.

A second later, she let go of him with a happy sigh and turned back to her trunk. "Why don't you see what we have in the kitchen while I unpack. I'm the best cook you've ever met, and I'd like to know what I have to work with."

It took her words a bit to translate in his head with the way his body was bursting to life. "Uh, sure. Whatever you want."

He turned to go, a supremely satisfied grin spreading across his kiss-heated lips.

"Shut the door on your way out," Eden called after him.

He thought nothing of it, still in a daze as he strode into the main room, the bedroom door clicking behind him. He took a few more steps, then stopped to take a deep breath. His stomach growled, as if it had been listening to Eden's talk of supper, but parts lower than that were close to driving him to distraction. He ached, pulsed, and itched to turn around, barge through the bedroom door, get rid of his clothes and hers, and do what married people did, trunk on the bed or no trunk on the bed. How long had he waited for this?

Luke was halfway through making up his mind to throw caution to the wind and make love to his wife when there was a knock on the front door. It made him jump a mile. Embarrassment struck him, as if whoever was on the other side of the door could see every lustful thought he was having. He glanced down at the front of his pants, and the awkward feeling intensified.

"Go down, go down," he whispered, then burst into laughter at himself. He shook his head and marched toward the door, working out how he could stand so he wasn't stupidly obvious to whomever was there to bother him.

Whoever it was knocked a second time as Luke reached the door and tugged it open. Travis Montrose stood on the other side, fist raised for another knock. He took one look at Luke and snorted into laughter.

"Am I interrupting?"

"Yes," Luke answered, crossing his arms, tempted to slam the door in his face.

Travis stepped into the house and thumped Luke on the back before he could, still chuckling. "Congratulations, partner."

"Thanks." Luke grinned, doing his best to pretend nothing was out of the ordinary below his belt. "I'm a lucky man."

"I'm sure you are." Travis cleared his throat to end his laughing and gave Luke's back one last thump before stepping away from him. "How is she?"

Luke's chest did a funny spasm, somewhere between

squeezing and thundering. "She's a dream," he answered. "Beautiful, spunky, full of fire and vinegar."

"Good. She'd have to be to put up with the likes of you."

Even that friendly ribbing couldn't dent Luke's good mood. "She's everything I could have asked for and more."

Travis's expression shifted to mischief. "So how do you think she'll feel about you heading out tomorrow to lead up the cattle drive?"

Shock dropped like a rock into Luke's gut, quickly followed by the sensation of pride and victory exploding through him. His jaw dropped, and it was a moment before he could form the words, "Really? You're going to let me lead the drive?" It didn't seem possible for one man to have as much luck as he was having that day.

"Franklin says you've earned it," Travis said, giving Luke an approving nod. "He's been impressed with the commitments you've made recently, that saloon fight notwithstanding."

"I swear, I won't let anything like that happen ever again. I just want to do a good job, prove myself, be a leader." Luke could have danced, his soul felt so light. Marrying Eden had worked. One little "I do," and he'd gotten both the promotion he'd been dying for and the promise of loving whenever he wanted it.

"Now, I should explain that for this first drive, you and I will be leading it together," Travis went on.

Luke's exaltation slipped by a hair. "Together?"

Travis held up his hands. "It's nothing personal. This is the way things are usually done. You're an experienced cattleman, but since you've never led a drive before and this one will be longer than the others we've done, you'll be shadowing me."

"Shadowing?" Maybe he'd started his celebration too soon.

"This time," Travis stressed. "Just in case we run into any problems."

Luke rocked back on his heels and studied his friend. Was he really being given the promotion he wanted so badly or not? It sounded a little to him like he was still under someone else. "Well, all right. If that's the way things are done."

"They are."

Travis opened his mouth to go on, but the bedroom door clicked open and Eden swept into the room. Luke's heart dropped to his feet at the sight of her. She'd taken off her traveling jacket and fluffed her hair up a bit, but she was the same gorgeous, spritely, bright-eyed wife that had left him in an embarrassing state ten minutes ago.

And she gave Travis a glance that was a little too appreciative, as far as Luke was concerned.

"Hello, who are you?" she asked, sashaying up to Luke's side.

Travis twitched into a grin that just kept growing and growing the more he looked at Eden. "I'm Travis Montrose. And you must be Mrs. Luke Chance." He held out a hand.

Eden took it, shook, and leaned forward to say, "That's *Eden* Chance to you." She even added a wink.

Luke's good mood thumped to the ground. He scowled. "Travis was just going."

"Was he?" Eden blinked innocent eyes up at Luke, clasping her hands behind her back.

"He was," Luke growled.

Damn him, Travis chuckled. "I was." He nodded to Eden. "Ma'am." Before turning, he winked at Luke. "Enjoy your wedding night. You've earned it."

Luke was caught between wanting to puff up his chest and gloat, and wanting to give Travis a black eye. It would do no good giving the man who he would be working so closely with for the next couple of weeks an injury, so he swallowed his jealousy and nodded as Travis shut the door. But Lord help him, if anyone ever looked at his wife like that again, he'd—

Eden stepped around in front of him, leaned against him, and threw her arms around his shoulders. "Sorry. I'm used to being friendly. It helps you get out of sticky situations."

She pushed up to her toes and planted another of those kisses that left him with no idea which direction was up on his lips. Before he knew it, he had his arms around her waist, pressing her close to his chest. The curve of her breasts tight against his chest felt like a dream, and her fingers playing in his hair were heaven.

When he got a chance to come up for air, he just had to ask, "Are you sure you weren't a whore before living at Hurst Home?"

As soon as the question was out, he mentally smacked himself upside the head, but Eden only laughed.

"I swear I was not." The shake of her body against his as she laughed had him worked up like a bull in spring. "But that doesn't mean I don't know which end of a mattress is which."

The sensation that he was about to crawl out of his skin if he didn't get her naked under him in short order slammed him again full force. "You'll have to show me." He bent toward her, eyes trained on her lips.

She gave him a quick peck, then wiggled out of his embrace. "Right after supper, sweetheart. I'm famished."

She danced around him, heading to the kitchen. Luke

stared after her. This was going to be the longest evening of his life.

Eden finished off her last bite of fried chicken, relaxed against the back of her chair, and signed with contentment.

"That was delicious." Luke echoed the substance of her sigh, resting a hand over his stomach.

"It's amazing what you can do when you have a full kitchen and adequate supplies." She'd just sit there for another minute, feeling full and content, then she'd clear away the plates. And then the fun would begin.

Luke's expression quirked to curiosity. "Did you not have enough to eat before you went to Hurst Home?"

Eden tapped her fingers against the edge of the table, wondering how much to tell her new husband and how fast. "Sometimes," she answered slowly. "Sometimes we have more than enough. Other times…" She shrugged. Life on the run could get tricky in a heartbeat.

Luke frowned, rubbing his chin and regarding her as if working out a puzzle. "You didn't work at a whorehouse, you don't have that sort of skittish look that Franklin's bride has, which makes me think you weren't beat on by anyone."

A pang of sorrow for Corva—and too many of the other girls she'd become friends with at Hurst Home—hit her heart. "I'd like to see a man try to raise a hand to me."

That brought a proud grin to Luke's face. "So why were you living at Hurst Home?"

Eden tilted her head to the side and studied Luke. Broad shoulders, strong arms, hesitant eyes. He'd been just jumpy enough during supper to hint he was waiting for "dessert." She could spill her story now, tell him all about her brothers, and run the risk of Brent's prediction that no man would want her for who she was being true, or she could get him out of those clothes and into their marriage bed, where he'd want her for other reasons. It'd been a while since she'd had fun with a man that way. Just maybe, if her luck held out, it could be more than just fun. She wasn't too proud to admit that she wanted it to be special, forever, with her husband, with Luke.

She made up her mind and pushed her chair back, standing and carrying her plate over to the counter with the sink. "I was in danger. Let's just say that."

Luke stood and carried his plate to the sink as well. "But how? I can't imagine a girl as tough as you being in any kind of danger at all."

She liked the grin that tweaked his lips when he said that. She liked the fond spark in his eyes. Some of her friends back at Hurst Home were loath to ask Mrs. Breashears to find them a husband because they believed there was no way a woman could love and trust a man at first sight. Well, Eden wasn't the kind to carry silly notions about love around, but the one thing life had taught her was that when a trustworthy man came along, you could tell in a heartbeat. It was about time she staked her claim to Luke Chance, heart, soul, and especially body.

"You know what's more dangerous than my reasons for being at Hurst Home?" She lowered her voice to a purr and swayed closer to Luke.

"Uh…" His jaw went slack and his eyes dropped right to where they should, her chest.

She played along, reaching up to undo the buttons of her blouse, opening it to show him the swell of her breasts straining against the top of her corset.

"The trouble we could get into." She finished her thought. "That's more dangerous. What do you say?"

There was an even chance that he didn't hear her

question. His eyes stayed fixed on her breasts as she unbuttoned the rest of her blouse and shrugged out of it, tossing it over one of the chairs at the small kitchen table. She followed that by unhooking her corset and shrugging out of it. Years of getting dressed and undressed on the run had enabled her to shed her clothes in a flash.

Luke's eyes widened as her breasts hung loose underneath her thin cotton chemise once her corset hit the floor. She grinned at him, standing boldly, shoulders thrown back to accentuate her chest. It was an invitation, and Luke took it up. He reached out, cupping one of her breasts in each hand. Lord, it felt good to have a man's hands on her. Big, strong hands. Shivers of anticipation for all the ways she could give in to this big, strong man and let him have his way with her, any way he liked, coursed through her, pooling between her legs.

But Luke just stood there, breathing hard, pupils dilated, holding her breasts. He didn't even brush his thumbs over her nipples or lean over to kiss or suckle them, or squeeze or do any of the things other men had done to play with her. Sure, the bulge in his trousers was growing by the second, but it was almost as if…as if…

"Luke, have you ever been with a woman before?" she asked in her kindest voice.

He remained frozen for a few more seconds before sucking in a breath and taking a half step back. His hands dropped to his sides. "No, ma'am."

Eden's heart blossomed in her chest, and the ache between her legs grew. "Why not?"

Luke blinked and met her eyes. A deep blush filled his face. "Well, that wouldn't be proper now, would it?"

She couldn't help but laugh, a low, throaty laugh that had him licking his lips. "I can't say I've met many men with enough honor and good sense to stay out of a woman's bed because it wouldn't be proper. Usually other things take over and honor flies out the window." She nodded to his trousers.

"My pa always said it was better to respect all women like they're someone else's wife and get acquainted with your hand than to do something you might regret," he blurted in one long breath, then added, "I'm very well acquainted with my hand."

He blinked and went beet-red, as if realizing what he'd said. Eden giggled, more charmed than she'd ever been in her life.

"Your pa sounds like a wise man."

Luke wiped a hand over the wince that'd come to his face. "He is. Look, that was a stupid thing to say, I'm—"

She cut him off by surging into him, throwing her arms around his neck and slanting her mouth over his. He was stunned at first as she traced her tongue along the line of his mouth, but a breath later he softened, parting her lips and joining her in a dance of tongues and passion. His arms slipped around her waist, then just as quickly, one hand moved up to hold her breast. Eden's heart sang, shooting desire through her. This was going to be her best night in a long time.

In short order, Luke lifted his other hand to cradle her breast, then broke their kiss to lean back and watch as he circled and squeezed her. He did more than just stare now, testing their weight, moving his thumbs and palms over her nipples until they were hard, and squeezing, all with rapt attention.

"They're just so wonderful," he answered an unspoken question in an awed voice.

"Never seen a pair before?" She tried her hardest not to giggle at his innocence and to respect his discovery.

"Seen? Yes," he admitted with a blush. "Touched? No."

"Well, here." She stepped back and drew her chemise up over her head, dropping it on the floor.

Passion flared in Luke's eyes as Eden leaned back against the counter, arms gripping the edge, to give him a good look. "I'm your wife now," she told him. "So you can look and touch as much as you like. You can even kiss them."

His eyes widened, as if the idea was new. Without words, he stepped closer to her, reaching to cradle her breasts once more. Only this time, he took her suggestion and bent to lay a soft kiss on top of one. The deep hum that swelled up from his chest had Eden gasping for breath, but not as much as his mouth as he shifted his kissing down to her nipple. When he closed his mouth around its stiffening point and sucked, she gasped so hard she lifted to her toes. Luke may not have had experience, but he had keen instincts. His tongue tasted her, laving until her nipple ached and she moaned in approval.

Luke inched back, peering up at her. "You like that?"

"Sweetheart," she panted, "I *love* that."

"Good," he answered with a rogue's grin and went back to work.

He pressed her breast up toward his mouth, alternately sucking—hard and soft—licking, and nipping with his teeth, as if working out what he liked best. Eden had to grip the edge of the counter as pleasure pooled between her legs, making her knees weak. If this was what Luke could manage on his first attempt, she shuddered to think what he could do to her with a little practice.

She did shudder when he switched to her other breast, sending a shot of cold air to her sensitive, damp nipple. His attention to that side only lasted for a few seconds before he stood straight and let out a shuddering breath.

"I feel like I'm about to burst," he told her in a low growl. "I think we should get to bed before it's too late."

"I think you're right," she replied, equally breathless.

They didn't wait. Luke took her hand and marched out of the kitchen, through the Hen House's main room, and into the bedroom, kicking the door shut behind them. He went straight to work on the buttons of his shirt and trousers.

Eden only had time for a quick glance around the room. She'd unpacked her trunk as fast as she could earlier, storing her few clothes and hiding all the things that needed to stay hidden until she had a chance to explain her past. Luke didn't appear to be in any mood to search under the bed or at the back of the drawers in the bureau as he tossed his shirt aside and shucked his pants, and Eden didn't care one way or another once he straightened and displayed all his naked, male glory to her.

"Good Lord." She pressed a hand to her pounding heart as she stared at the size of his penis. It stood thick and tall, at full attention, tip gleaming with moisture, ready to go.

A flash of self-consciousness pinched Luke's desire-flushed face. "You don't like it?"

Eden reached for the back of her skirt, fumbling to undo the fastenings so she could get naked as fast as possible. "Sweetie, I'm gonna ride that like a green-broke stallion."

She dropped her skirts as she finished, stepping out of her damp drawers as fast as she could and launching at him. Luke's eyes widened and darkened at the split-second view of her fully naked that he got before she threw herself against him. He backpedaled until he hit the bureau. She covered his grunt of surprise with a mad-capped kiss, humming at the sensation of her body pressed fully against his. He was hot, his skin soft with sweat, enough hair on his chest to mark him as a man without keeping her skin from brushing against his. That wasn't all she wanted, though.

She reached between their bodies, closing a hand around his length. Her body quivered in anticipation as she stroked him, imagining how sweetly he would stretch her. Her nether regions practically begged her to crawl up on him and sheath him inside so she could feel it. Heaven help her, she was going to scream in all the best ways once he got to the point where he had control.

Control that he wouldn't have if this was his first time. The thought cooled her by a fraction, and she leaned back, moving her hands to his hips. Sure enough, he was breathing heavily after just a little bit of play. There was no sense in pushing him to the edge before he learned what to do once he got there.

"Come on, sweetie," she whispered instead. "That bed isn't gonna warm itself."

"Yes, ma'am," he growled.

She gave him the moment of respite that he didn't know he needed by pushing away and turning to walk seductively around to the far side of the bed. He looked at all the right things, her pale backside, the sway of her hips, her thighs, as she walked. She swallowed a laugh as his hand flinched toward his cock. Well, it was what he was used to, after all. Maybe once they got comfortable with each other, she would let him pleasure himself while looking at her. Although why eat gristle when you could enjoy a flank steak?

She threw back the bedcovers from the far side of the bed. "You coming?"

He didn't wait another second. Before she could climb all the way into bed, he launched himself between the sheets. Their bodies met—hot and ready—in the middle of the cool sheets. Luke groaned as he stretched beside, her, wrapping his arms and a leg around her. One hand went straight for her breast and his mouth sought hers out in a kiss that made up in passion what it lacked in finesse.

There were still a few lessons her new husband had to learn before she would let him run wild, though. Eden clasped his hand over her breast and drew it down over her side and stomach, through her thatch of curls, and on to the wetness between her thighs. He hummed in surprise and delight, and she gasped when he tightened his hand around her mons. The sensation of him claiming that part of her as his—even though he didn't know that's what he was doing by holding her so possessively—sent electric sparks across Eden's skin.

She pivoted to her back and opened her legs as much as she could in their current position. Keeping her hand over his, she guided his fingers deeper into her cleft, steering him to the parts of her that were desperate for his touch. He was a quick study, and as his fingers found her opening and his middle finger delved inside of her, they both gasped.

"That's you," he whispered, unsteady.

She could only hum in response. At the risk of him thinking she was a wanton trollop, she ground her hips against his hand. His finger inside of her sparked delicious pleasure, but as she writhed and wiggled against him, she shamelessly positioned the calloused pad of his hand directly against her clitoris, pressing her hand hard on top of his to keep him where she wanted him and to increase the pressure.

She was already so worked up that it only took a few seconds of grinding against his hand to send her into thundering waves of pleasure. It was so good that she cried out, pressing his hand over her harder as she bore down on his finger inside of her. Luke groaned and panted, and when she opened her eyes as the intense pleasure gave way to deep, floating sensuality, she saw his expression set in wide-eyed shock.

He worked his mouth, not finding any words to say.

Eden grinned with satisfaction and reached up to stroke his face with her free hand. "You like that?"

His hand—still firmly wrapped around her sex—twitched. "Mmm hmm," he managed.

"Me too." She sighed and shifted, pivoting her hips to signal him to move his hand, then sliding under him. "Now it's your turn."

No more words were needed. He knew exactly what she meant. His body went hard with longing over top of her. His hips jerked against hers, anticipating what carnal instinct prompted him to do. Eden toyed with the idea of drawing things out, teaching him a little more about what their bodies could do, and heightening the pleasure they could feel, but the fierceness in Luke's eyes told her he needed completion, and fast. They had years, a whole lifetime, to draw things out and drive each other crazy with lust.

She wriggled her hips under him, opening her legs and drawing her knees up to his sides. He ground his hips as well, and she gasped as, once again, she was reminded how large he was. Her pulse sped up at the thought, and she stretched her hips as wide as she could to give him the room he'd need. In a flash, she was aching with the need to be his body's shelter and the home for his passion.

He struggled against her, breathing hard as his hands found purchase on either side of her. She rested her hands on his hips, panting with expectation as he stroked and nudged her. It wasn't until the movements had gone on a little too long that she realized he wasn't sure how to find her entrance. A wave of emotion so tender it stung her eyes swept over her, and she reached down to take him in hand. He stilled, his body rock-hard at her touch, then she guided him to where he needed to be.

They both breathed in as his tip slid inside of her, her path found and ready. She let go, and his instinct took over. With a low roar, he jerked forward, sinking deep inside of her. She cried out wordlessly as his size stretched her, right up to the edge of pain without reaching it. He was magnificent. She wanted to grip the bedsheets and let him pound away in her until she found her release again as the object of his pleasure, but he still needed her.

He rocked back, ready for another thrust, and nearly slipped right out of her. She hummed, gripping his backside with her full strength to stop him from pulling back too much. He thrust again, a long groan accompanying the motion, then rocked back. Again, she stopped him before he could go too far. Forward and back, faster and faster. She gave her full attention to feeling him, not to take her pleasure, but to make sure he found his as smoothly as possible.

His groans turned into a long series of ragged, wolf-like rumbles as he lost himself to the rhythm they created together, faster and harder and primal. She knew he was close when his muscles began to tighten, and when his groin and backside clenched in time to a long cry of pleasure that flared excitement through her, she knew he'd spilled his seed inside of her. She'd never let any man do that before, no matter how good they were. That was for Luke and Luke alone.

With a few more sated thrusts, he stilled and collapsed on top of her, completely spent. Grinning from ear to ear, Eden rolled him to the side, keeping her leg thrown over his hip and his shrinking length inside of her. It felt so uncommonly good that she didn't fight the laugh that bubbled up from her gut.

"What?" Luke panted, an edge of worry in his voice, even as his arms closed around her.

"I was just thinking," she said. "You're mine now, whole and complete, and we get to do this whenever we want to from now on."

He blinked, held his breath, and then he pressed his head back against the pillow and laughed in triumph.

As morning sunlight filtered through the curtains in the windows of the Hen House, Eden drew in a deep, contented sigh. Coming awake to find herself in bed next to a handsome man who was her husband was better than being in a dream. If she wasn't careful, she might just lose her heart to the beauty of that safe, strong man. She stretched, humming, then curled herself around Luke's well-muscled body. A body, it turned out, he knew how to use. Whether he had any experience or not, he'd known just how to move, just how to kiss, and with a little guidance, just how to make her feel like the luckiest woman alive, last night. Several times.

And here Brent had told her that no man would ever want her. Well, her brothers were hundreds of miles away now. Brent's threats meant nothing. They could risk their lives and shoot up as many banks as they wanted. She was free of them forever, safe in the arms of a real man. Brent didn't have the first clue where she was.

Eden was close to drifting back to sleep on the cloud of joy that those thoughts brought her when Luke stirred. He flexed his muscles, groaned as if some of them were sore, then lifted a hand to rub the sleep from his eyes. Eden grinned and snuggled closer to him, thinking to herself, "Mine, all mine."

For a moment, Luke held his breath. Then he puffed it out in a hurry and sat bolt-upright.

"What time is it?" he hissed.

Only a little concerned—her brother Braden used to wake from a sound sleep and jerk to his feet, looking for trouble, before he was all the way awake—Eden rested a hand on his back. "I don't know, sweetie. There doesn't appear to be a clock in here."

Luke only grunted at her answer, jumping out of bed and dashing over to the bureau. Eden nestled back against the pillows, drinking her fill of his powerful body as he yanked open the top drawer of the bureau and started pulling out clothes, sniffing them to make sure they were clean. The broad lines of his back and thighs were beautiful, and the curve of his backside and dangly bits in front had her biting her lip.

He was halfway through tugging his trousers up when he glanced to her. He froze, raking her with a sultry gaze. She hadn't bothered pulling up the bedcovers to hide herself when he leapt out of bed, and was more than a little pleased at the sight she presented to him.

"Where are you going in such a hurry?" She propped herself up on one arm, giving him a "come hither" stare.

Luke's jaw fell open. That was a finer reaction than the most flowery compliment he could have come up with. Well, that and the way certain dangly parts of him twitched to attention. Eden laughed low in her throat, shifting to her back, fully expecting her new husband to change his mind and rejoin her in bed.

Instead, Luke shook his head and tugged his pants up with a wince. He fastened them, then threw his shirt over his shoulders. He did a few buttons, then strode over to the bed, bending over to plant a kiss full of longing square on Eden's mouth. She reached for him, but he straightened and took a step back.

He rubbed his face, breathed out a heavy sigh. "I had no idea it would be this hard."

Eden's mouth twitched and her eyes dropped to his trousers. It would be too easy to twist his words into a teasing comment. "What would be hard, sweetie?" She opted for a straight question instead.

"Leaving you."

Eden's grin dropped, and with it every bit of humor and contentment she'd enjoyed a moment before. "What?"

Luke growled like a wolf torn between attack and retreat. He rubbed his stubbly chin and shifted from one foot to the other as he watched her, brow furrowed. The longer Eden stared at him, the worse his struggle seemed to be. Where in heaven's name did that sort of torment and guilt come from?

Her silent question was answered a second later when Luke said, "I've got a cattle drive to lead."

Eden blinked. "A cattle drive?"

"Yeah." Luke continued to sway in his spot, grimacing as if he was being pulled apart. "I didn't realize how much I'd want to stay."

"Then stay," she said, voice flat.

He leaned toward her, then snapped back, shaking his head. As he marched around the foot of the bed to the door, he said, "I can't. I got people depending on me. This is my big chance."

"Big chance for what?" Eden leapt out of bed, ignoring her state of undress, and followed him to the main room.

"My big chance for the promotion I've been trying for

all year." He gathered his boots from the middle of the floor, where they'd ended up last night, and sank into the sofa to put them on.

"What, right now?" Eden planted her fists on her hips, sure she looked a sight.

Luke glanced longingly at her, his flush deepening as his eyes lingered on her breasts, but he force himself to concentrate on getting his boots on, then stood and strode to the rack where a leather vest hung.

"I've been working on Howard Haskell's ranch since I got here when I was seventeen years old," he explained. "I learned the business, learned all there is to know about cattle. I was hoping I'd move to a position where I could do more, lead men, a couple of years ago, but Howard hired the Montrose brothers instead. They had more experience running things, but I knew I could be in charge too."

"So, why aren't you?" As far as Eden was concerned, her husband was a natural leader.

Luke shrugged and winced, marching toward the door where his hat hung on a peg. "Franklin said he wasn't convinced I was serious enough. I told him I'd prove I was." He nodded to her.

Eden opened her mouth to make a comment about how ridiculous it was for anyone to think he was anything but serious. She stopped. The truth dawned on her. He'd sent away for her to prove he was serious. She clamped her mouth shut, not sure if she was offended by that or if Luke was damn clever to think of it.

She shook her head to clear away that conflict. "And you have to leave right this very instant or you'll never get a second chance to move up?"

She meant her comment to be sarcastic, but Luke answered, "Yep," with dead certainty. "I'm sorry that I had to marry you and run. I'll be back in a couple of weeks. If all goes well, sooner."

That was it. With a sharp nod, he turned and scrambled out through the door. It banged shut behind him.

"Well, I'll be a turkey's tail feather," Eden cursed under her breath. She sank her weight to one hip and shook her head. That was it? That was all the explanation he had to offer?

She wasn't going to stand around and take that. With a burst of energy, she rushed back into the bedroom. It would be worse if Luke abandoned her the day after their wedding without a care. At least he had looked troubled about it. That would keep her from slapping him into next Sunday when she caught up with him.

She splashed water from the pitcher on a side table into its matching bowl, soaked a cloth, and went to work washing up as fast as she could. Her mind bustled with calculations. It couldn't take that long to get everyone organized for a cattle drive. They'd seen the cattle themselves waiting in the field the day before. Chances were that the whole operation was ready to set out. This wasn't the first time she'd had to jump into action with no time to spare.

It was a good thing she'd unpacked and put everything away just so the day before. She threw open the middle drawer of the bureau and pulled out the narrow, split skirt she used to wear when riding with her brothers and tossed it on the bed along with a simple blouse, a chemise, and drawers. There was no time for a corset on the open range, and in truth, she was tired of wearing one just to fit in.

She dressed in less than a minute, then dropped to a crouch and reached under the bed. Good thing Luke had been too busy with everything going on *in* the bed to question if she'd hidden anything *under* it. She slid out the long, heavy, flat case that had been at the bottom of her trunk and moved it to the jumbled and bunched bedcovers on top of the bed.

With a quick glance around to make extra sure no one was watching, she flipped open the case. A grin spread across her face at the sight of her old friend, her Winchester Model 1873 repeating rifle, with its twenty-four inch octagonal barrel that she'd had inscribed last year.

"Hello, you beauty," she hummed to it, lifting it out of the case, kissing the casing.

With swift, sure hands, she clicked it open, checked the magazine. Everything was still clean as a whistle. There were plenty of bullets in her case, but rather than load the rifle, she transferred a couple of boxes to the hidden pockets in her skirt. She set the Winchester down for a minute while she drew her gun belt—with its pair of Colt Peacemakers—out and fastened it around her waist. Lord, it felt good to have that weight across her hips again.

The last thing she did before snatching up her Winchester and rushing out the door was to braid her hair. She could brush it later. Right now, time was all that mattered. Time and the fact that there was no way in hell she was going to let her new husband leave her alone in the Hen House for a couple of weeks right after marrying her.

Luke shook his head as he marched into the paddock where his horse stood waiting along with the others. Travis and the boys were deep into preparations for the drive. Franklin Haskell sat atop his horse—where he was most mobile—overseeing everything and answering questions. It was uncanny how every last thing he'd ever been told about women suddenly made sense all at once. They were sweeter than honey and could make a man lose his head. They were the most frustrating creatures God ever invented, but a man couldn't live without one. There was no sensation more right and more glorious than having a woman wrapped around you while you sheathed yourself inside of her.

But more than everything else, he suddenly understood how a woman could be a man's sweetest source of joy and his most acute source of pain. As much as he'd wanted to hop back in bed with Eden that morning in an attempt to figure out how many times a man could lose himself in one day without passing out—or, hell, dying—he had a job to do.

"Told you you should have waited until after the drive to send for that wife of yours," Mason Montrose ribbed him as Luke reached to help him saddle the horses.

"Shut up," Luke growled. "Franklin wouldn't have let me lead this drive if I hadn't sent for her when I did."

"What makes you say that?" There was humor in Mason's voice.

Luke took it as teasing. Worse than teasing, laughing. He scrunched his face into a defensive frown and shot his friend a sour look. He was surprised to find Mason grinning at him with nothing more than friendly ribbing and a touch of genuine concern.

Still, Luke went ahead and said, "I know what you all think of me."

Mason's expression twitched to confusion as he threw a saddle blanket over Cody's horse, Buford. "What do we think of you?"

Luke grunted. He fetched Travis's saddle from the rack and walked it across to Archer, Travis's horse. He would have let the question drop, but as he tightened the buckles, he noticed Mason standing and staring at him with crossed arms.

Maybe Mason wasn't laughing at him, but Luke wasn't going to take being stared at and judged lying down. He straightened. "You all think I'm only good at leading saloon fights and card games, that I'm too much of a fool to take on any real responsibility."

Mason chuckled and shook his head. "No, Cody's the fool who can't handle responsibility." He headed for the rack of saddles, slapping Luke's arm as he went. "You just can't handle your liquor."

Luke wasn't sure if that was friendly teasing or an insult. Either way, he turned to Mason, intent on defending himself.

He stopped cold at the vision of Eden marching into the yard beside the corral. His jaw dropped at the sight of her—slim skirt that kicked like trousers when she walked, her dusty travel jacket, a belt with two revolvers on her hips, and a well-worn Winchester slung over her shoulder. All those heady, carnal feelings he'd had in her arms last night slammed back into him like riding a horse plumb into a wall.

"Luke Chance," she hollered, searching around. Luke jerked straight, and when she saw him, her eyes narrowed. She stomped toward him, demanding, "What the *hell* makes you think you can traipse out of here without me the day after marrying me?"

Hot and cold rushed through Luke at once. Mason nearly dropped the saddle he'd hefted into his arms, and his eyes went wide. Across the corral, Cody and Travis, Billy and Lawson stopped what they were doing and gaped. Franklin turned his horse so he could see what was going on too.

Luke gave Travis's saddle strap one last tug, then quick-stepped over to his wife. "What are you doing here?" he whispered.

"We just got married." She didn't bother to keep her voice down. "I'm not letting you out of my sight."

Luke ran a hand through his hair. He noticed Travis leaving what he was doing to march toward them, and Franklin nudging his horse to join them. Just what he needed, the men he was trying to prove something to witnessing him getting dressed down by his wife.

"I've got a job to do, Eden," Luke rushed on, trying to get things taken care of before anyone else got involved.

"I understand that, sweetheart," she said, far more gentle than he expected. "But I've got a job too—that of being your wife."

"Which means you stay at home and cook and clean and make things pretty, right?" His brow shot up in desperate pleading as both Travis and Franklin reached them.

"Morning, gentlemen." Eden greeted the two with a winning smile.

"Mrs. Chance." Franklin touched the brim of his hat. "At least, I assume you're Mrs. Chance."

"I am, and proud of it," Eden answered before Luke had a chance to explain.

That last bit left him tingling with affection and at a complete loss of how to handle things. "Eden just came to see us off," he fumbled.

She didn't contradict him, but neither did she agree. "I was actually hoping I might come along with you boys."

Luke flinched. "Come along with us? On the drive?"

"Yep." Eden nodded.

Franklin and Travis exchanged uncertain looks. "You

ever been on a cattle drive before, ma'am?" Travis asked.

"Nope," Eden answered.

She shifted her Winchester to her other shoulder, sweeping one side of her jacket back and cocking her hips so that her revolver stood out. Lord have mercy, she was wearing a Colt Peacemaker. Two of them. Luke swallowed. Who had he married anyhow?

"Mighty fine weapons you've got there, Mrs. Chance," Travis went on. "I take it you've used them before."

"Yes, I have," Eden answered with a smile.

The air itself paused to hear what else she would say about it, but Eden remained mum.

Franklin cleared his throat. "Mrs. Chance, do you really want to spend two or three weeks away from civilization, sleeping on the rough ground at night, eating out of a tin can, and dealing with a bunch of messy, smelly, ill-mannered…" He paused, glanced at his men, who had gathered to watch the scene, grinned, and finished with, "Cattle?"

Eden clearly caught what he's meant to say. Her grin matched Franklin's as she said, "Yep."

"Why?" Travis asked, crossing his arms.

Eden looked at him as though he were dense. "Because I just got married, and I want to be with my husband. What's so unusual about that?"

Her question was a dare. Travis and Franklin, and the rest of the ranch hands, squirmed and shifted, rubbing their necks and chins and whatever else they could to delay answering her. Luke only smiled, something warm and pulsing growing in his chest. He'd never met a woman like Eden before—never met anyone so fearless and bold…and possibly a little bit crazy. And she was his, wedded and bedded.

- that's what she meant about being friendly to get out of

"I'm not going anywhere unless Eden comes with me," he blurted, surprised that he meant it so vehemently. The other men stared at him. "You don't realize half of what this woman is capable of," he went on. "Neither do I, if truth be told, but I sure do want to find out."

Lawson leaned over and whispered something to Cody at the edge of the scene. Cody snorted. Billy and Oscar—one of Mrs. Piedmont's men who was coming along to help out—exchanged glances that said they just wanted to see what would happen next.

Travis glanced to Mason, then at Franklin with a shrug. "It's up to you, boss."

Luke darted a glance to Eden to see what she thought of that. She stood her ground, a confident grin on her pretty face, as if her inclusion on the drive was a foregone conclusion.

Franklin studied her. His expression twitched from an unreadable frown to an amused grin. "I'm newly married myself," he said. "And I can't imagine how I'd feel if I had to leave Corva for weeks on end."

"Corva's a gem among women." Eden nodded. "She was always one of my favorites at Hurst Home, always helping the other girls out. She offered to paint my portrait once, but for…various reasons, I declined." The shifty look that popped to Eden's face sent Luke's thoughts racing. He didn't have time to give it much thought, though. Eden went on with, "Tell Corva I say hello next time you see her."

Atop his horse, Franklin looked as though he'd been given a prize for valor. He nodded to Eden and said, "I will. I'm sure she'll want to catch up with you once you get back."

It was all Luke could do not to laugh out loud. So that's what she meant about being friendly to get out of sticky situations. Eden had to be the most clever woman he'd ever met, on top of the most beautiful and most sensual. She'd worked magic around Franklin Haskell, knowing exactly what to say to get what she wanted.

"I appreciate that, sir." She nodded respectfully to him, knowing she'd won. "And I promise to keep a sharp eye on your messy, smelly, ill-mannered *cattle* in the meantime."

Luke chuckled, heart light. At least, it was light until they started moving, figuring out which spare horse they could bring along for Eden. All that cleverness of his wife's could easily be directed at him any moment. He was going to have to watch himself where she was concerned. But then, that was another thing he'd always heard about women that he suspected he was about to find out was true. Men thought they wore the pants in their marriages, but women were the ones who sewed those pants, and they could make them as tight as they wanted.

Chapter Six

Eight hours later, Luke's heart wasn't so light. In fact, he felt as though a fifty-pound buzzard had crept up on his shoulder and was staring down at his every move.

"Watch the left flank," Travis called across the milling herd of cattle as they rounded a bend where a slope met the stream a few miles outside of Paradise Ranch.

Luke sat straighter in the saddle, glad at least that he felt as one with Marshall, his gelding. He spotted a pair of cows that looked more interested in investigating the slope than continuing on with the others. Instinct kicked in, and he nudged Marshall to investigate.

"No, no!"

A numb prickle crawled down Luke's spine at Travis's correcting shout. What had he done wrong? Anxious and frustrated, he turned Marshall toward Travis, who was now riding through the ambling herd to reach Luke.

"What?" Luke called when Travis got close enough. "I was just going to stop those two from getting away."

He glanced over his shoulder. Not only were the two cows still straying, Eden had paused atop her horse to watch him. Her face was shaded by the wide brim of her hat, so he couldn't tell what she thought.

Travis rode close, evidently keeping his reply to himself until he could deliver it face-to-face. Perfect. Luke grunted. His wife was about to witness him being reprimanded when he was supposed to be proving how competent he was. Just what he needed.

"You're trail boss," Travis said when he was only a couple feet from Luke. His horse danced, but Travis kept it under control. "Your job is not to herd the cattle, it's to herd the men."

"Yeah?" Luke tried to sound casual, but his mind raced to drink in the lesson, and his muscles clenched with the need to perform well.

Travis nodded. "So as leader, you can't do every job yourself. You see what needs to be done, who is available to do it, and you delegate to them."

"Right." Luke lifted to search over the dusty herd and the men from Paradise Ranch who were driving it. Cody and Mike were up at the front, pacing the cattle, Mike taking his turn driving the chuck wagon. Billy and Mason were over on the right flank. Lawson and Oscar rode drag, bringing up the rear. That left him and Travis…and Eden.

As if she could sense the conclusion he came to before he came to it, Eden smiled.

"She wanted to come," Travis said, seeing that she was the closest one to where action was needed too. He shrugged. "So far, she's pulled her weight. Why not put her to work doing something other than cooking?"

Luke gaped. "You want me to order my wife to bring back two straying cows?"

"Why not?" Travis nodded, a grin making its way into his eyes. "A good leader can train anyone to do any job." He was close enough to reach out and thump Luke's arm. "Go to it."

Travis rode off, and Luke nudged Marshall to move on. Eden must have sensed some of what the conversation had been about. She had already walked her horse along the flank toward the spot where the two cows were drifting further and further up the slope. Following them was one thing, but Luke had never seen a woman herd a cow.

He had, however, seen plenty of women herd a pack of unruly children. There was only one way to find out if that instinct stretched across the animal kingdom. Although, if he made a mash of teaching Eden how to manage cattle, he'd be reminded of it every day when he looked in her pretty face.

"No way to find out but to try," he murmured to himself, then kicked Marshall into action. "Hey, Eden!"

She pulled on her mount's reins to turn him toward Luke. "Hey, what?"

"Travis wants me to show you how to keep unruly cows from wandering off."

"*Travis* wants that?" A grin twitched her lips.

Luke frowned. "Yeah. That a problem?"

Eden shrugged. "Don't *you* want to show me how to rein in some cows, trail boss?"

Luke's mouth sagged open. "What's the difference?"

She chuckled. "There's a world of difference, sweetheart. You've got just as much backbone as Travis Montrose does."

"I've—" Luke frowned and shook his head. His plucky wife was driving at something, but right then there wasn't time to work it out. The pair of cows decided to make a break for it.

Luke pushed the strange conversation aside and

nudged Marshall, nodding to Eden, then ahead at the cows. She spurred her horse after him, and in no time, the two of them were riding wide of the herd.

"Cows aren't the brightest creatures God made," he explained as he showed Eden what to do. "They prefer to be in a mass. They like being guided. They get all itchy and confused when they stray."

"Kind of like a man?" Eden teased with a wink.

It was probably a jab at him, but Luke laughed anyhow. "If you'd like. All they need is a little gentle encouragement to head back to the path they're supposed to be on."

"Exactly like a man," Eden laughed. "Show me how?"

It shouldn't have, but that simple question puffed Luke's chest with pride. Sprightly as Eden was, she was asking for his instruction. He knew full well what he was doing and the best way to get it done, so as soon as she was shadowing him, he demonstrated the best way to guide and holler and coax nervous cows away from their escape plan and back into the bulk of the herd. Sure enough, as soon as they sensed their buddies around them, the cows gentled and their steps relaxed into the plodding lope of the rest of the herd.

"That wasn't so hard." Eden drew her horse up alongside his. Her chest rose and fell beautifully as she panted from exertion and concentration. Out in the sun, the dusting of freckles across her cheeks seemed more pronounced and downright...kissable. "You're right, it just takes some calling and nudging, and they go right back to where they want to be."

"In a situation like this, yes." Luke nodded, working hard to focus on the job instead of all the other things they could be doing. "If they end up in a full-on stampede or if there's some other danger, it's a whole different problem to solve."

"So how do you solve it?" She looked up at him like a student ready to be instructed by a master.

Something warm and bolstering flooded Luke's chest. "Well." He shrugged as though it was no big deal. "If they start stampeding in earnest, the first thing you've got to do is make sure there's no major source of danger in the immediate area, no cliffs or rivers or such."

"Uh huh. Then what?"

"Turn them to the right."

"The right?" She balked, smiling as though he was joking.

"I'm serious. Get them to turn to the right and start running in a circle. Once they get all balled up, they'll stop."

"By running to the right?"

Luke shrugged. "Cattle don't like turning to the left when they're running."

Eden burst into giggles. "That's the silliest thing I've ever heard."

"Well, it's true."

"Oh, I believe you, but still."

Off to the right, Travis called out, "Luke, watch your tail."

Luke twisted to check behind him. Another couple of cows had veered off, but only by a bit. He turned back to Eden. "Think you can handle them?"

"I know I can." She nodded, then wheeled her horse around to go after the strays.

The rest of the day passed in far more pleasant a manner than Luke ever would have imagined. The weather was holding, the herd was calm, and Eden was much more of a help than he could have imagined. By some miracle, his first day as a trail boss was going well. Pete, his adopted pa, would be proud. He even slept well when they set up their bedrolls and lay down under the canopy of stars. Eden camped out close to him, and crazy though it was, Luke was kind of glad she didn't try to climb in his bedroll with him. With all his buddies around, that would have been about as awkward as things got.

Morning dawned clear and cooler than days had been. Eden got up before the men—well, all the men except for Travis—and had a load of bacon and a pot of beans cooking over the campfire as everyone else came awake. The scent alone was divine.

"You sure did pick a winner," Mason said around a mouthful of breakfast as they prepared for the morning's work.

"Maybe you should think about getting married yourself," Eden answered his praise. "I knew a lot of girls back in Nashville who would love a life out here."

Mason shrugged. "I can't say as I'm ready to tie myself down yet."

"Why?" Cody snorted. "What are you doing that requires not being tied down?"

Mason flushed. "Well, I could go off on an adventure any day."

Cody laughed. Even Travis shook his head. "If Luke here can settle down with a woman, than anyone can," he said.

Luke frowned. "What's that supposed to mean?"

"Come on." Mike thumped him in the arm from his seat beside him by the campfire. "You've never exactly been the serious and responsible type."

Before Luke could protest and insist that he was as responsible as any of the others, Cody rushed on with, "Well I'm sending away for a wife. I already told Mrs.

Evans I wanted one the other day, right Luke?"

"And what did she say?" Mason drawled, as if he knew the answer.

Cody's enthusiasm faltered. "She said she'd think about it." He hopped up, face more than a little red, and marched his dishes over to Eden.

One by one, the men finished their breakfast and got down to the business of cleaning up camp and saddling their horses. Eden tidied up breakfast and stored things away in the supply wagon. Whether because he was embarrassed or just because it was his turn, Cody volunteered to drive the wagon for the day. Luke thought about asking Travis if Eden could have more time to clean up their food, but by the time he thought of it, Eden already had everything stored and secure and the fire doused and covered in dirt.

"Where'd you learn to clean a camp that fast?" he asked her as the two of them rode on the right flank an hour later.

"From my brothers," Eden answered.

That was all she answered. There was nothing wrong with that explanation, but now that Luke had spent some time with his new wife, he was beginning to see that sometimes she didn't look him in the eye when she told him something. Nothing else gave him the idea that she was uncomfortable, but the more he looked, the more that didn't seem normal.

He had more cause to doubt as the sun rose to its zenith above them.

A commotion rose up from the cattle on the left flank. Luke and Eden both twisted and craned their necks to see what was going on. Billy managed to keep the cows on the left flank from spooking, but his shout of "Coyote! Coyote on the left!" set everyone on edge.

"Steer the herd away from it," Luke called out on instinct, nudging Marshall into a faster walk.

"Keep them moving," Travis echoed him from the front.

"I've got it."

Luke pulled his horse to a stop in surprise at his wife's call. He twisted to check on where he'd left her behind him, only to find her reaching for her rifle. She'd stored it in her saddle, and as soon as it was in her hands, she checked the magazine and raised it to aim so fast Luke could only blink.

Eden stood in her stirrups, drew in a breath, and narrowed her eyes. The rifle cracked as she fired a shot. Her horse jolted, but she moved as though she hardly noticed. Far across the other side of the herd, fifty yards away at least, a cloud of dust and shower of splinters filled the air as her bullet hit its mark dead center.

"That's no coyote," she shouted to the others.

"It's some sort of dead log," Travis agreed, then laughed. "You seeing things, Billy?"

The tension that had gripped them all dissolved into chuckles and teasing.

"It looked like a coyote," Billy grumbled.

Whether it looked like a coyote or a log or an elephant, Luke was captivated by something else entirely. He slowed his horse, waiting for Eden to catch up. She still held her rifle…as if it was perfectly at home in her hands.

"Oh, wife of mine," he began with a crooked grin. "Where did you learn to shoot like that?"

She shrugged, and once again answered, "From my brothers."

Her eyes wandered out over the herd, brow knit in concentration. Luke saw it as the ploy it was. Curiosity bubbled through him like a stream after a storm.

"So, if you have brothers who were willing to teach you so much about surviving, how come you were in a home for women in danger?" he asked with a sly grin and narrowed eyes.

For the first time in the tumultuous thirty-six hours since they'd met, his wife blushed and stammered. "Well…I…sometimes a woman wants to be around other women and not a bunch of rough and stinky men." That explanation bled right into, "Watch out, someone's trying to get away."

She nudged her mount to hurry after a cow that might have looked in the wrong direction, but who was in no more danger of straying than Luke was.

Luke rubbed his face, trying to decide if he should be alarmed or amused. It was too late now for him to give a fig about what Eden's life had been before Hurst Home. He'd already married her, and she was proving to be exactly what he wanted. But he sure did wish she'd come out and tell him who these brothers of hers were.

Well, damn. The last thing Eden expected was to feel bashful about telling her new husband the truth. After a quick lunch, they hit the trail again. Travis had moved Luke to the back of the herd and spent a half hour imparting wisdom about what a leader looked for from that position. Eden shifted into position with them, but her mind was a thousand miles away.

She should have known better than to draw her rifle and show off her shooting. If she'd just waited a few more minutes, someone else would have seen that the "coyote" was a log, and she could have ridden on, cool as you please. But no, it'd been so long since she'd felt the smooth grain of wood encasing that cool, metal barrel that she couldn't resist its siren call. But that wasn't half as alarming as the way she'd gone all squirrely when Luke started asking her questions.

If Luke knew the truth about her family, about who she'd been before escaping to Hurst Home, he wouldn't like it. If he didn't like that, he wouldn't like her. He'd either pull away and spend the rest of his life resenting the fact that he'd married someone who misrepresented herself, or he'd get rid of her entirely. And Lord help her, she liked Luke. A lot. Which meant she wanted him to like her. *A lot.*

"*Stop being such a girl,*" Brent's voice echoed in her head.

She frowned and clenched her jaw, nudging her horse to ride up beside Luke's. Brent was hundreds of miles away. He didn't know where she was. Even if he did, if he had managed to trace her to Hurst Home somehow, what could he possibly do about it? No, she was free of him and that life forever.

"Once you get your eye for the position, you'll be able to spot trouble before it happens and direct your men to cut it off before it develops into anything." Travis was still instructing Luke.

Luke nodded with intense concentration. "I got it."

Eden had no doubt that he did. His shoulders were set and the angle of his chin as he scanned the herd was the picture of confidence. Eden's heart thrummed with promise, knowing that he was her husband…and it shivered with worry over whether she would lose him for things that had happened years before meeting him.

Luke's intent gaze tripped across her as he assessed the cattle, and he smiled. Smiled like a bullet shot clean through to her heart.

"Enjoying yourself?" he asked, maneuvering his horse so he could ride closer to her.

"In every way." She did everything she could to look carefree.

"Were you paying attention to everything Travis said about riding back here in drag position?" He nodded to Travis, who still rode only a few yards away.

"Nope," Eden admitted proudly. "I was too busy watching you."

Luke blushed and lowered his head a tad. "Shucks, ma'am," he teased.

He opened his mouth to say more, but from the left flank, a call of, "So, is Travis teaching Eden to be a trail boss now?" from Cody stopped him.

Luke frowned and sat higher in his saddle. "Show some respect," he called back.

But before he finished, Billy was already adding, "Seems to me like Mrs. Chance would make a mighty fine boss."

Billy and Cody laughed. Luke's jaw hardened to the point where knives could be sharpened on it. He scowled like a thunderstorm.

"Never mind them," Travis said, shaking his head.

Easier said than done, especially when Mike and Mason caught on from the right flank.

"I'd take orders from Eden any day," Mike shouted with a laugh.

"Why, because she's prettier than Luke?" Mason asked, loud enough for everyone to hear.

"No, because she's tougher than him."

Luke's shoulders sagged and his expression drooped as the other cowhands burst into guffaws. The men riding point turned in their saddles to see what was going on, but, blessedly, didn't get involved. Eden was sorely tempted to draw her revolvers and offer to shoot the next man who made a disparaging comment about her husband, but it would only have proved the point of the joke.

"I'll go talk to them," Travis said and nudged his horse to trot off to the left flank.

"You don't—" Luke tried to stop him, but gave up. He let out a string of colorful curses under his breath.

Of all things, that made Eden smile. "Well, I'll be, Luke Chance. What an amazing vocabulary you have."

He glanced to her, shoulders still down, with only a wisp of a grin.

"Oh boy," Eden sighed to herself. She inched her horse closer to Luke's and touched his arm. "Why the hell do you care what they think anyhow? They're just a bunch of dumb cowpokes."

Luke sent her a look that was so mournful she was tempted to laugh. "If they're just a bunch of dumb cowpokes, then so am I."

"I beg to differ."

He arched a brow, staring at her with a wary look that said he assumed she was pulling his leg.

Eden hissed out a breath and shook her head. "Why let them get to you? You're the one who was chosen to learn to be a trail boss, not any of them. And from what I've seen over the last few days, you know what you're doing and then some."

Luke shook his head, but halfway through a dismissive gesture, he stopped and stared at her for a long time. Eden could practically see the gears turning in his head before he let out a breath and said, "Half the time, I'm not sure if I really do know what I'm doing or if I'm just stumbling along, making things up."

Eden had spent enough time around her brothers and their egos to know that Luke had just handed her the most precious gift he had to give, his pride. The importance of giving a good answer, an answer that would help her husband feel like a man, pressed down on her.

"Everything I've learned about you in the last two days tells me that you're a fine man with a solid head on his shoulders," she said. "Am I right?"

Luke winced. He slipped his hat off, wiped the sweat and dust from his brow with his sleeve, then put his hat back on. Finally, he answered. "As long as I can remember, I've been getting into trouble. I thought it was my job to keep the adults from thinking they could control me or hurt my family."

"That's right noble of you." Eden nodded.

He glanced sideways at her in surprise. "Then, one day, I woke up and realized I *was* the adult. Only, everyone around me still expects me to get into trouble and cause a ruckus."

"That doesn't mean you're actually a troublemaker or a...a ruckus-causer."

"Exactly," he barked, as if arguing the point. Then he let out a sigh. "But do you ever get folks telling you you're one thing for so long that even though you know you're not, you're not sure who or what you actually are?"

Eden thought of her brother, Brent. She thought of the midnight escapes and the heists. She thought of scouting out towns and climbing up to the roofs of buildings with her rifle to cover her brothers when they snatched the loot and ran. Most of all, she thought of the pistol that had been cocked and aimed at her head when she put her foot down and told Brent she didn't want to be like him anymore. She'd walked out in spite of his threats, banking on the fact that he wouldn't come after her. He wouldn't. She kept telling herself that.

"Yes," she answered, barely above a whisper. "I know exactly how that feels."

Luke shook his head, unable to see the turmoil of her past. "Sometimes I wonder if I really am capable of being a leader or if God planted me here on this earth to be…entertainment."

The way he said it, the sorrow and defeat in his eyes as he considered the path he felt forced to walk, lit a fire in Eden's gut that reached up and grabbed her heart. She'd felt forced to walk her path too, until she risked her life to run from Brent. It was the least these stupid, blind cowpokes with cow pies for brains could do to respect a man for realizing he could do better than be a joke. Luke had competence in spades. She admired him for it more than she would have guessed she would when she met him, and she could feel that admiration growing into something more.

"I tell you what," she said with all the force of fire behind her words. "Any man who doesn't see that you're a born leader is a crying fool."

Luke balked, but his back straightened. "You think so?"

"Sweetie, I know so," she insisted. "From the second I stepped off that train, you've been arranging things and facing things head on and doing the jobs you're meant to do, as a rancher and as a husband."

A hint of a smile pulled at the corner of his mouth, and this time it stayed there. "Well, the husband things were a might easier than the rancher things." The blush that kissed his cheeks was a reflection of the heated mischief that came to his eyes.

"And I know you'll continue to fulfill those particular duties to the very best of your ability."

He chuckled, his blush deepening. "Kinda makes me wish we weren't out on a drive right now."

She giggled—giggled like a schoolgirl. Lord, it felt

good to let herself get swept up in something as ordinary as being sweet on a man. Not just a man, her husband.

"Next time you get to feeling like those lard-for-brains fools expect you to act like one of them, just remember you've got at least one person who thinks you're the king of the castle."

He puffed up with such pride at her simple comment that Eden's throat squeezed tight.

"I appreciate that," he said, voice gruff with emotion. "I can't say there've been many people who showed that kind of faith in me."

She grinned. "I can't say I've met that many people who I've wanted to believe in."

He glanced sideways at her, his grin tightening. For a moment, Eden worried she'd said too much. Luke narrowed his eyes, deep in thought.

At last, he said, "You sure you're only just looking to be a rancher's wife and mother of his children?"

She let out a breath on a laugh. "Sweetheart, you have no idea." She wanted to be a *safe* wife and mother. Her eyes danced off across the herd, over the wilderness that they walked through, at the other cowhands. Anywhere but at Luke.

Luke hummed as though figuring out a puzzle. "One of these days, maybe you'll put all your trust in me instead of just some of it."

His words were quiet, thoughtful, and they stung. He knew she was holding back. Dammit, now she'd have to work out a way to tell him about her past. She just needed to find a way to do it that didn't end with him hating her.

Chapter Seven

In spite of the fact that Eden wanted nothing more than to settle down with a constant roof over her head, steady food on the table, and enough safety to bring babies into the world, as the next few days passed on the cattle drive, she enjoyed herself. There was a world of difference between riding out with her brothers—always hiding, always looking over her shoulder—and ambling along with Howard Haskell's ranch hands, a clear job to do in front of them.

The best part of all was the time she got to spend with Luke.

"You gonna eat that last piece of bacon?" she asked, nudging his shoulder as they sat side-by-side around the breakfast campfire.

"Of course," Luke replied, in good humor. Eden made a move to snatch the bacon from his plate, but he was faster. He swiped it up and chomped on it before she could do more than laugh.

Lord above, it was nice to have an easy, free relationship with a man. A good relationship, one that was proper and aboveboard. The cattle drive gave her a chance to get to know her new husband in a way she never would have if he'd gone off to work every day while she stayed home. She liked what she was learning. In fact, she'd venture to say she was falling hard.

The two of them continued to nudge each other and giggle like disobedient kids in a school room, until Travis crossed behind them on his way to pick out a fresh horse for the day from the remuda, the herd of saddle-broken horses they had brought with them on the drive to give the other horses a rest now and then.

"Breakfast should be squared away and we should all be ready to go in fifteen minutes," Travis said in passing.

"Yes, boss." Luke jumped to his feet, taking his last bite of bacon with him.

Eden hopped up after him, setting about gathering the breakfast dishes that the ranch hands had left behind. "You're the boss too, you know," she chuckled.

She expected Luke to make some sort of snappy comeback, but instead he sighed as he stamped out the campfire.

Eden frowned and straightened, her arms full of tin dishes. "What?"

Luke was slow to look at her. His silly mood had vanished in a blink. He scowled at the ashes of the fire as he stamped with a little too much enthusiasm. Eden took her armful of dishes to the back of the chuck wagon, where Lawson, who drew the short straw and had wagon duty for the day, was setting things in order. She dumped the dishes there, then marched back to Luke, crossing her arms when she reached him.

"Spill it, cowpoke," she ordered him.

Her teasing at least managed to wipe the scowl from Luke's face and replace it with a fond smile. Eden enjoyed the shivery thrill that smile gave her, but she wasn't after flattery at the moment. She continued to stare at her husband, arms crossed, brow arched to underscore her question.

At last, Luke gave up with a sigh and stepped closer to her. "I'm supposed to be learning how to lead a cattle drive, right?"

"Right."

Luke shrugged, a thread of anger working its way into his downtrodden expression. "So how come, three days in, Travis is still giving all the orders? He showed me how to run all the positions, told me a lot of stuff I already know about cattle."

"Yeah?" Eden shifted her arms to rest her hands on her hips, leaning closer to him in support.

"The only reason I can think that he hasn't turned over more authority to me is that he doesn't think I deserve it in the first place," Luke said at last.

The spark of anger in his eyes over the situation caught hold in her. "That's not right. Maybe he's the sort of man who has a hard time letting anyone else take the lead." Heaven knew her brother Brent was that kind of man, as they'd all learned far too many times.

"Yeah, well…" Luke rubbed the back of his neck, grimacing. Then he sighed and let his arms drop. "Nothing I can do about it now except do my job. And maybe talk to Franklin when we get home."

"Maybe," Eden echoed with a nod. She gave Luke an encouraging smile.

He returned that smile, then marched off to get his job done. Eden continued cleaning up the camp, but the entire situation didn't sit well with her. Yes, she'd learned a lot in the last few days, but not everything she'd learned was adding up. Travis not letting Luke take the lead, the other ranch hands poking fun at him every chance they got, Luke's slips in confidence. Something had to be done.

Once their camp was cleaned up and the men were busy saddling their horses and organizing the herd, Eden marched over to Travis.

"I want to talk to you," she began straight out.

Travis was about to mount his horse, but stopped and twisted to face her. "What can I do for you, Mrs. Chance?" His lips twitched as if he thought calling her that was funny.

Eden wasn't amused. She crossed her arms and asked, "Why aren't you giving my husband more responsibility? You're supposed to be teaching him to lead a cattle drive."

Travis's grin dropped, and his jaw with it. "Well, ma'am, I am teaching him."

"Mmm hmm." She continued to stare him down, as if they were about to march twenty paces and draw. "So why haven't you given him the chance to take the lead for a while."

"Well…I…uh…"

"And furthermore, why are you letting the other men continue to make jokes at Luke's expense?"

"Jokes? Um…I hadn't noticed any—"

"Men don't treat other men as a leader if they're allowed to make jokes about him," Eden stormed on. "You all keep bringing up that saloon fight he was involved in and his escapades at Bonnie's—which I happen to know for a fact are pure fabrications," she added. Travis opened his mouth, but she rode over him with, "Franklin Haskell wants Luke to learn to be a trail boss. As far as I understand, he's in charge of you all. So, you tell me why you aren't following his orders."

Travis stood frozen, staring at her. She knew it was a wily move, but she settled her weight on one leg, sweeping back the corner of her jacket to show off her Peacemaker as she planted a hand on that hip. Travis blanched.

"All right, I accept that you may have a point," he muttered.

Eden grinned. "Good."

Travis looked up to meet her eyes. "Why didn't Luke come to me himself? Why did he send you?"

Damn. She hadn't thought about that. It didn't look great when a man's wife defended him to his boss. "He thinks he can handle things himself," she said, willing to make herself look like a loose cannon as long as Luke got the respect he deserved.

It was Travis's turn to cross his arms and hum, "Mmm hmm. So this wasn't his idea."

Eden winced. "Not exactly."

Travis stepped closer to her. "I'll tell you the truth, Mrs. Chance." This time he didn't say her married name as if it was a joke. "Luke is a good worker, but he doesn't exactly have the best track record with dependability."

Eden wanted to snap back a reply, but she kept her lips sealed.

"You haven't known him that long, but I'll admit that he's been well-behaved since you showed up," Travis went on. "He could be a fine trail boss, but he lacks confidence."

"Not as much as you think," she said.

Travis shrugged. "You're here talking to me, not him. That says something."

She opened her mouth to argue, but this time it was Travis's turn to cut her off.

"I'm more than happy to help Luke do whatever he wants to do, but he needs to have the confidence to come to me and ask. Understand?"

Unfortunately, Eden did. "Yes," she grumbled. She couldn't leave it at that. "The least you could do is give him the opportunity to come forward and show his confidence."

She squared her shoulders, looking Travis straight in the eye to show him she wasn't intimidated by him contradicting her. Travis held her gaze for longer than was strictly proper. Then he nodded—a nod full of respect. That was something, at least.

"I'll do my part if he does his," he said.

Eden nodded to him one last time, then turned to search for her horse. Several yards away, across the abandoned camp and the dust that had been kicked up by the herd as it started to move, Luke sat atop his mount, watching her with a scowl. Eden peeked over her shoulder at Travis as he too mounted up. Lord help her, but if that was jealousy in Luke's eyes she'd have to knock some sense into him.

Then again, it might not have been the best idea to talk to his boss without checking with him first.

"Yee-ah! Get a move on there! Cody, watch out for the runners on your right," Luke called across the rumbling herd as they walked around a particularly treacherous turn at the bottom of a low hill.

"Huh? Oh, right," Cody called back. He nudged his horse to chase after the potential strays.

Luke ground his teeth at the way Cody had been so slow to respond. He'd been grinding his teeth since that morning when he saw Eden talking to Travis. The two of them had stood a little too close, spoken far too intensely over something. It was bad enough that his foray into leadership wasn't going so well, but to have his wife whispering away with another man, a stronger, bolder man? She'd been awful nice to Travis when he came to the Hen House the other day, no matter why she said she'd done that.

He swallowed the sour taste at the back of his throat. Women sure did have a way of turning your world topsy-turvy. If Eden had been Mrs. Piedmont or Lucy Faraday or Corva Haskell or any other woman from town chatting with Travis, he wouldn't have given it a second thought. But Eden was his wife, and whether he liked it or not, seeing her talking to another man made him grumble like a bear. That wasn't a quality a leader should have either.

"Whoa, whoa, keep up back there," Travis shouted from point position as they cleared the curve and led the herd on to the next plain.

Luke twisted to check over his shoulder. Eden was riding drag with Billy and Mike, and doing as fine a job as the men. That much brought a reluctant smile to his parched lips. He was proud of her, proud of her strength, her smarts, and the fact that she hadn't complained once since they'd hit the trail. Granted, he was sure the past she hadn't yet told him about was the reason she was so tough, and he couldn't decide if he wanted to know everything about it or nothing at all, but he was still proud.

Which looped him back around to the conversation she'd had with Travis.

Luke let out a frustrated sigh. A woman as intrepid as Eden should be with a man who had grit, who possessed a steel backbone and iron balls. Was he that man? Was he man enough for her? He thought back to their wedding night. It had been his first time with a woman, and he figured he'd done a good enough job, judging by the sounds Eden had made. But a niggling thought at the back of his mind figured she'd had as much to do with that as he did. Hell, he hadn't known the first thing about what he was doing, but she did.

She did.

He winced and rubbed his face and eyes to push away the headache that was forming. What if Eden decided she'd rather have a man who knew what he was doing in bed, in life, in everything? What if she ended up wanting Travis instead of him?

"You look like you're about to puke, sweetheart."

Her voice right behind him jolted Luke so hard he nearly slipped out of his saddle.

"Whoa there." she chuckled. "I didn't mean to startle you. I didn't think I *would* startle you either."

"I was thinking," he admitted, fighting not to feel sheepish over his thoughts. They were legitimate thoughts, possible concerns. He didn't have to feel guilty about thinking them.

Then why was he being so defensive with himself?

"Good." Eden nodded, thankfully oblivious to the riot going on inside his head. "I like a man who thinks."

"Do you like a man who takes charge and is respected by his peers too?" he grumbled before he could stop himself.

Eden hissed out a heavy sigh, shaking her head. "Don't go counting your chickens before you look hard enough to realize they're ducks."

The metaphor was so strange that Luke laughed in spite of himself. The fact that Eden could make him laugh when he was wallowing in self-consciousness only made him want her more.

A real man, a man worthy of Eden, would speak out and not sit on the burrs of his doubts.

"What were you talking to Travis about?" he asked, working not to look jealous and stupid.

To his surprise, Eden blushed. "I might have gone and chewed him out for not giving you more responsibility."

Luke's brow flew up. "You chewed out Travis? Over me?

"Now, before you get all upset at me for taking things into my own hands," she rushed to defend herself, nudging her horse to ride right up next to his, "I just want to let you know that I only did it because I think you deserve more credit. I should have let you take the lead, though. I'm sorry."

Luke was so flabbergasted—by her honesty and by her gumption—that he stared at her in silence as they rode on. The herd was already spreading out across the plain to munch on the parched grass. Travis signaled from the front for them all to stop for lunch, and Luke waved back. He wheeled his horse around to check on the tail end of the herd. Mike raised his shoulders in question, and Luke gestured for him to follow the direction of the herd so they could camp for a few hours.

It was several minutes before he had a chance to react to Eden's statement as the two of them walked their horses to the stream where Lawson was setting up lunch.

"You know." He began slowly so that he could sort out the jumble of his thoughts. "I can think of maybe three people who have ever gone out of their way to defend me in my life."

"Really?" Eden seemed genuinely surprised beside him.

Luke nodded. "My ma—my real ma, before she died—Josephine, and my big sister, Libby." He smiled as he thought of all three of them and turned to Eden. "I always thought it was funny how the only people who ever saw something in me were women."

Eden's answering smile was so soft and feminine—almost as if she had tears in her eyes—that it tightened his throat.

"It's because women are smarter than men," she said, leaning closer.

"You know, Mrs. Chance, I think you might be right." He winked at her, hoping she would take it to mean that he had no hard feelings about her talking to Travis. Why the hell had he thought she would take a shine to Travis in the first place?

Because he wanted her so much that the very idea of her turning to someone else was almost more painful than he could bear.

He sucked in a breath. Whoa. No wonder love was compared to Cupid firing an arrow. It hit you that fast and stuck that hard.

They reached the edge of the quickly thrown-together camp. Luke hid his sudden burst of feeling by dismounting. Getting skewered by Cupid's arrow was one thing, but if Eden didn't feel the same about him, it would be more of a wound than a wonder.

He busied himself getting Marshall settled and helping Eden with her horse. Only when he had gathered his calm enough to look strong and commanding did he whisper to her, "I appreciate your help, Eden. I really do. I only hope I can live up to your expectations."

She stepped closer, lifted to her toes, and kissed his lips. "You will," she said and patted his cheek before stepping away to help Lawson with lunch.

Cody and Billy hooted and made kissing sounds at him. "Want us to rope off an area so the two of you can be alone?" Cody laughed.

"We could clear out the back of the wagon for a

while," Billy added. "Just don't go rocking hard enough to break the wheels."

They snorted with laughter. A few of the others reluctantly joined in. Eden frowned.

"That's enough of that." Travis stepped in, his voice commanding. "Show some respect."

Cody and Billy's teasing expressions faltered. They glanced to Luke, as if expecting him to go along with his teasing, to open himself up to being the butt of jokes.

Luke settled into an easy stance, tipping his hat back and grinning like he knew something they didn't. "I might have to take you up on that offer." He winked across to Eden, who grinned and blushed and shook her head. Cody and Billy continued to gape, so of course Luke leaned closer to them and said, "Jealous, boys?"

To everyone's surprise, neither Cody nor Billy had a ready comeback. There was a first time for everything.

"Well, we all know who the smart one here is," Mason added as he took a bowl from Lawson and served himself cold beans from a pot. "I bet we're all wishing we had sent off for brides ourselves."

Lawson laughed at the comment and started around the camp, handing out tin bowls to everyone. Cody and Billy not only kept silent, they edged around Luke with the averted looks and hangdog expressions that men only wore when they worried they'd gone too far and offended someone they shouldn't.

Luke grinned. Hope filled his chest as he helped himself to a lunch of cold beans and cornbread. If he wasn't mistaken, he'd just taken the first small step to being a real leader.

"Good job," Eden whispered as she sat next to him on the ground beside the chuck wagon.

"You think so?" He leaned into her, bumping his shoulder against hers.

"Yep." She nudged him back.

Luke couldn't remember the last time he'd been happier. Things were looking up.

Lunch was unusually quiet, almost as if the boys didn't know what to say if they didn't have Luke to tease. It wasn't until Mason suddenly frowned and squinted back the way they'd come that the mood shifted.

"Who's that?" he asked.

They all turned to look back at the hill they'd just come around. It was a couple hundred yards away, but a lone figure on horseback stood out against the western sky. Luke squinted, trying to see far enough to tell if he recognized the rider.

"Must be a scout from a local ranch," Travis said.

"I didn't think there were any ranches out this far," Luke said.

"Could be an Indian?" Lawson ventured.

"No." Travis shook his head. "He's not dressed right."

"You can tell from this far away?" Cody asked.

"I bet it's one of Bonneville's men following us," Mrs. Piedmont's man, Oscar, said.

The others hummed in agreement, standing and setting aside their lunch to glare at the lone rider.

"Bonneville," Luke growled. He balled his hands into fists, ready for another fight.

But no, a leader didn't lead his men into pointless altercations.

"What do you want to bet Bonneville is sending his men out to sabotage the drive?" Lawson grumbled.

Travis sighed. "I wouldn't put it past him."

"As if sabotaging dealings with Dashiell wasn't bad enough," Mason grumbled.

Something shiny flashed near the rider's head. "What's that?" Billy asked.

They all shifted, shielding their eyes to look harder. The flash appeared again, then disappeared as the lone rider lowered his arms. Luke scratched his head as some of the other boys shrugged and returned to their lunch.

"Bonneville can eat my dust," Billy muttered.

"It's a spyglass."

Eden spoke so quietly that no one but Luke paid her any mind.

"A what?" he asked.

When he turned back to face his wife, his heart dropped to his feet. She'd gone as pale as a sheet and held her bowl of beans as though they would make her sick. Her stance had changed too, and now she sat half curled up in a ball, as if she could fold up and disappear.

Luke jerked back to stare at the hilltop, but the rider was gone. Something hard and primal rose up in his gut. He squatted by Eden's side, setting his bowl aside.

"What is it? What's wrong?" He closed his hands around her arms, caught between wanting to hold her close and needing to chase after whatever had frightened her—and she *was* frightened—and destroy it.

"It's a spyglass," she repeated, voice shaking, eyes round with dread. "He always carries that damn spyglass."

Chapter Eight

Three times in the next day and a half, Luke checked for burrs in his saddle. The itching, stabbing sensation that something was very wrong refused to leave him, even after Eden brushed away her comment about the spyglass, busied herself cleaning up lunch, and pretended nothing was out of the ordinary. The others hadn't noticed her discomfort or heard her comment, but it wouldn't leave Luke. Of course there were no burrs in his saddle, but he would have preferred that answer to the dangerous tension that floated all around him.

"Ho! Ho, there, Luke!"

At Travis's call, Luke snapped out of his prickly thoughts. Jumped was more like it. His heart raced as he twisted in his saddle to find Travis. Off to the right flank, a single cow was drifting to the side, but Eden was there to guide it back in line. He hadn't noticed the cow making a break for it. He hadn't noticed anything.

"Yeah?" he called across to Travis, barely able to be heard above the noise of the cattle.

From point position, Travis glanced back at him with a frown. He held back until Luke rode up around the herd's right flank. Along the way, he sent Eden a look that was as steady and reassuring as he could manage. He would protect her from whoever that was on the hill. He would keep her safe, make her happy.

"What do you want, boss?" he asked Travis as Marshall fell into step with Travis's mount.

"I want you to get your head out of the clouds," Travis got right to it. His frown lightened to deeper concern. "You haven't had your head on straight since we saw Bonneville's man on the hill yesterday."

Luke opened his mouth to say he doubted that had been Bonneville's man, but closed it just as quickly. He didn't know who the man was and wouldn't until Eden opened up to him.

Travis went on. "Look, I know that saloon fight was a crossroads of sorts for you. I admire the changes you've been trying to make. But if we get into a tussle with Bonneville's idiots out here on the drive, it won't be a fool's fight, like at The Silver Dollar. You'll be defending the herd. No one is going to think less of you for that."

Luke turned about three shades of red—from embarrassment to anger—at Travis's speech. Travis was a friend and was trying to show support, but he still didn't think much of him. He could argue the point, but that would only draw Eden into things, and she was upset enough already.

"Yep," he answered, his jaw set, his eyes trained straight forward to the curve of the river they were approaching. It was all the answer he could give.

Travis studied him in silence. Luke knew the man to be smart enough to catch on to all the unspoken stuff that was going on, but he wasn't going to be the one to speak first. Finally, after a long, awkward silence, Travis nodded and let out a breath. "We'll reach that river in about twenty minutes. The herd has to ford it. I want you to lead while they do."

Surprise bumped Luke straight out of the gristmill of his thoughts. "Me?"

Travis quirked to a grin. "That's why you're here, aren't you? To lead?"

Thank God above for Eden. Maybe her little chit-chat with Travis had done some good after all. "Hell yes." He smiled, the first smile that felt natural in two days.

"All right." Travis faced forward, nodding chin-first at the line of the river. "I'm pretty sure this is Dyson's Run. It's a little narrower down this way. Ride on ahead to see how deep it is and where would be the best place for the herd to cross."

"Yes, sir." Luke nodded, then tapped Marshall to send him running ahead of the group. It felt good to gallop, to feel the wind in his face, his muscles working in tandem with his horse. It felt good to have a specific purpose and a task ahead of him that was more than worrying and wondering. He could do this.

The river was more of a stream as far out on the plains as they were. Luke rode right into it, slowing Marshall enough to test the riverbed, looking for submerged obstacles, depth, and speed of the water. Every lesson he'd learned about cattle and the wilderness in the past ten years and more came back to him, like well-oiled cogs in a machine. He remembered crossing rivers as an adolescent on the Oregon Trail. Sometimes they'd had rafts to take them across, but for smaller streams like this, they'd waded through. He remembered the advice Pete had given him with a confident smile.

As he galloped back to Travis and the herd, his mind was full of calculations and a sense of purpose. Travis rode out ahead of the herd to meet him. Luke pulled

Marshall to a stop and waited, scanning the dusty cloud of the herd for Eden. She still rode on the right flank, but judging by the stoop of her shoulders and the angle of her hat brim, she wasn't paying any more attention than he had been.

"What does it look like?" Travis asked.

"I think we can—" Luke stopped cold. Before he could turn back to Travis, his eyes caught something far in back of the herd—a flash of light. He stood in his stirrups, squinting to see if he could make it out.

"What?" Travis turned his horse to look where Luke was looking.

"I thought I saw a flash of light," he said. "Like the one we saw yesterday."

"That reflection from Bonneville's man," Travis said.

Luke swallowed. "Yeah." His heart hardened and he clenched his hands into fists around his reins.

Eden must have seen him searching for something, because she had stiffened from her defeated posture and was looking over her shoulder. The last thing Luke wanted was for her to worry more than she already was. He gave up searching behind them and focused on the task in front of them.

"There's a nice, sandy, shallow spot right over that way." He pointed across the plain in front of them as the herd plodded closer. "Should be easy enough to cross, as long as none of the cattle strays too far downstream toward those rapids."

He went on to explain the lay of the land on the other side and the depth of the stream. Travis nodded with confidence.

"Sounds like you've got this figured out," he said with a smile. "Take the herd across."

Of all the times for Travis to hand the reins over to

him with a hearty vote of confidence, it had to come at exactly the moment when Luke would have rather abandoned his duties to chase after whatever was upsetting his wife. This was his moment to shine, and suddenly his thoughts were everywhere else. He clenched his jaw, tightened his grip on his reins, and nodded to Travis. A true leader finished the job in front of them, no matter what the distraction. If he could get the herd across quickly and efficiently, then he would have more time to devote to solving Eden's problems.

"Right." He sat taller and waved to the others. "Lead the herd this way. There's a good spot to cross between those trees and that pile of rocks," he shouted.

He shouldn't have been so surprised that Mason and Cody and the other who had had no problem poking fun at him a few days before waved and hollered back and went exactly where he pointed them. The herd shifted its course, slowly marching on to the ideal river crossing. It was as hard to believe as it was thrilling that everything was falling into place. Luke breathed in the proud sensation of leadership, but only for a moment. He had a job to do.

When the first of the cattle splashed into the river, right after Mike drove the chuck wagon across, he was there to guide them across. The ruckus that the herd made walking across land was nothing to the splashing and lowing and thunder they made as they forded the river. As the front of the herd ran up onto the opposite bank, water splashed everywhere, making the far side of the river a muddy mess. Luke directed Mason and Travis to continue on at point as the thick of the herd gamboled across the current.

"Keep them away from anything farther downriver than those bushes," he ordered Eden and Billy as the middle of the herd clogged the river. "There are rocks starting about that point, and the water gets deeper."

"Yes, boss," Billy replied without question.

That simple acknowledgement was almost as heady as Eden's proud smile as she rode up to his side. "I knew you had it in you," she said, eyes flashing.

Lord above, nothing on earth felt as good as the approval of a man's wife. At that moment, he felt like he could drive all the world's cattle across the Amazon River. He felt like he could carry a cow or two on his back up to the mountain peaks in the distance. He felt like he could—

Another flash of reflected light jerked him toward the horizon behind them. He walked Marshall to the side, squinted and studied the horizon. It took all his willpower not to charge after the light. The riverbed was too low to see anything, but that flash was unmistakable.

"What is it? What do you see?" Eden asked, too breathless for his liking.

The last thing he wanted to do was answer her fears. "A flash," he admitted, dragging his gaze from the horizon to meet hers. "I won't let anything happen to you."

She met his declaration with a weak smile. "I know."

"I'm serious, Eden. Whatever that is, I will protect you with my life."

"Whoa! Whoa there! Stray!"

Luke jerked at the sound of Billy's call just in time to see one of the cattle who had strayed too far downstream losing its footing. It lowed in fear and splashed before slipping under the water.

Luke didn't wait. He wheeled Marshall around and ran through the unsteady water as fast as he could to reach the cow. Marshall faltered when they hit the rocks, and Luke was forced to slow down and take it easy. The struggling cow thrashed and screamed, but it didn't lose its footing entirely.

"Easy there, girl, easy," Luke called out to it. He fought against the current and guided Marshall over the rocky riverbed as carefully as he could. The rocks were intermittent in this part of the river, but a few more yards downstream and not only would the cow be lost, he and Marshall might find themselves in danger too. Time was of the essence.

"It's okay, girl, it's okay." He pushed Marshall forward until they stood between the cow and the rockier riverbed. As soon as he was close enough, he reached out and touched the cow's neck. It wasn't much, but the simple gesture served to point the cow in the right direction and let it know it wasn't alone.

From there, Luke walked Marshall diagonally through the current and upstream. The cow was reluctant at first, but as soon as it was able to take two steps through the chest-deep water without hitting stones, its confidence grew. Within minutes, it changed course and made straight for the rest of the herd as they crossed in the smoother section of river. Another minute later, and Luke and the cow were charging up the far side of the river onto the muddy plain on the other side, drenched by unharmed. Luke's pulse pounded and his hands shook slightly, but they'd made it.

It would have been far easier for Eden to enjoy the celebration in Luke's honor after the river crossing that evening if it weren't for the creeping, pernicious fear that had her wanting to pick up everything and run. She couldn't have been prouder of Luke, and was happy that he was getting his due at last. But every snap of a twig and every rustling critter in the bushes had her gasping and jumping. Brent had made good on his threat. Somehow, he'd found her.

"And did you see the way he just reached over and touched the cow's back?" Billy laughed, telling the story yet again from his angle. "It was like he had some sort of power over the dumb thing to make it calm down and get back in line."

Luke blushed and smirked as his buddies sang his praises. "It was nothing. The poor cow was frightened and just needed to be pointed in the right direction."

"Yeah, but you didn't see how close to the edge of those rapids you were?" Mason went on. "One wrong step and it would have been disaster."

The others hummed and nodded in agreement as they finished off the fried chicken Eden had made to mark the occasion. She could barely eat. The men were right— Luke had come heart-stoppingly close to hitting the rapids, and who knows what would have happened then.

"And then he comes up on the riverbank with that stoic expression and says 'Everyone all right?'" Billy went on with his story.

The others chuckled and guffawed. Oscar was close enough to thump Luke on the back.

Eden smiled at the praise Luke was getting for half a second before the shriek of a night bird somewhere across the plain sent her blood running cold. She hid her nerves by standing and collecting everyone's empty dishes.

"You should have been close enough to see the expression on his face," Billy went on.

Eden tuned him out. She carried an armful of tin plates to the chuck wagon and began cleaning them out with a greasy, old rag. Her eyes kept darting toward the horizon behind them. Night was falling fast, but she was still able to make out most shapes against the backdrop of

the river—now a hundred yards behind them or more—
and the plain and mountains beyond. There weren't many
hills or much vegetation in this part of Wyoming, but that
didn't mean Brent and the others couldn't find a place to
hide. In fact, they had always been able to hide, whether
there was cover or not.

"Everything all right there, Mrs. Chance?" Cody
asked, saying her name with respect instead of teasing this
time.

"Huh?" Eden dragged her eyes away from the
horizon. "Yeah. Fine." She turned back to the chuck
wagon and the task at hand.

"I'd love to see Bonneville's men try and ambush us
now," Mike said. Eden's ears pricked. The topic of the
conversation had changed.

"Yeah," Cody agreed. "They think they can be all sly
and sneak up on us way out here? Well, we got the best
team of ranch hands and cow pokes this side of Denver."

"What did you say?" Eden snapped to attention,
nearly dropping the plate in her hand in her haste to
search the western horizon once more.

"That we've got the best team this side of Denver,"
Cody repeated.

The shapes along the horizon took on a menacing feel
as Eden narrowed her eyes at them. She had her rifle only
a few yards away in her bedroll, and her Peacemakers
were still holstered at her hips, but if Brent and the boys
were close, that might not be enough. "Before that," she
whispered.

The pause that followed was uncomfortable. A few of
the men exchanged uncertain glances, half of them
directed at Luke.

"Only that whoever Bonneville sent after us to muck

up the drive, they don't stand a chance of sneaking up on us," Billy said.

"There was only one," Eden whispered, throat closing by the second.

"No, ma'am," Mason said in the same tone a ranch hand would use to soothe a skittish cow. "There were three of them about an hour ago."

"What?" Eden yelped. How could she have missed them? Her heart thundered against her ribs.

Luke stood and walked to her side. His expression was firm and commanding, and he rested a steady hand against her shoulder. "You were cooking supper. We didn't want to upset you."

Her mouth went dry as she glanced up at him. She swayed closer to him, wanting to hide in his arms as much as she wanted to turn and draw her revolvers to fight. She'd spent far too long standing and fighting. You couldn't stand and fight against Brent anyhow. They'd all learned that the hard way.

"Hey." Luke lowered his voice to a tender caress, cradling her face. "Whoever that is, I won't let them touch a hair on your head. You're mine, and I take that responsibility seriously."

As beautiful as it was to see Luke's newfound confidence, and as tenderly as his words wrapped around her heart, Eden still wanted to weep. She'd never been a weeper. In fact, she'd made fun of weepy girls since she was two steps out of the cradle. It made her sick to feel so vulnerable, but that's what had driven her to Hurst Home in the first place.

"I know," she whispered, doing her best to bolster her confidence. "And I won't let anyone or anything hurt you either."

She lifted to her toes to plant a light kiss on his lips. Behind them, a few of the boys whistled and catcalled. Any other day, Eden would have given the lot of them black eyes, but in that moment, their teasing warmed her heart. They were there too. Brent might have been on her tail—and she was certain it was him after seeing the flash from his spyglass—but she had a new gang now.

"Need help cleaning up?" Luke asked, brow raised.

She wanted to tell him to go away and let her do her job on her own, but having him close was too much of a comfort. "Sure," she said. "You scrape off these plates while I store what food you ravenous beasts didn't eat."

It felt good to joke, good to rag on the men that had fast become her friends. The camp settled into companionable chatter as the sun went down. Mike pulled out a harmonica, and Billy a mouth harp, and the boys settled into soothing cattle drive songs. Eden and Luke finished cleaning up supper by the time the last light in the sky faded behind the mountains.

"Come on," Luke whispered to her while the others were distracted. "Grab your bedroll and we'll turn in for the night."

There was a glimmer in his eyes that Eden would have seen on the darkest night. She planted her fists on her hips and hissed, "Luke Chance, there are half a dozen men only yards away wherever we lay our heads."

Luke answered with a guilty chuckle. "Okay, so we can't actually do anything." He swaggered closer to her—peeking around to make sure the chuck wagon shadowed them from any roving attention—and swept her into his arms. "That doesn't mean we can't enjoy a little kissing and cuddling."

He ended his statement with a kiss that lifted Eden off her toes. His body was large and encompassing around her. His hands held her with a firmness and command that she was more than willing to surrender to. His lips played with hers, and his tongue teased between them, exploring and tasting. It was such a relief that Eden risked sighing aloud and pressing closer to him.

"Uh, you two need some privacy?" Lawson called from the far side of the campfire. His question was followed by chuckles and sniggers.

Luke broke their kiss, but kept Eden in his arms. "Let's set our bedrolls up at the other end of the camp from those yahoos."

Eden couldn't help but giggle and go along. She marched back to the camp to collect her things, sticking her tongue out at the men who winked and chuckled and made faces at her and Luke. Let them think whatever they would. Men were funny. If the boys thought she and Luke were getting up to mischief that night, it would probably raise their estimation of Luke even higher.

"I'll set them straight if you want," Luke told her once they found a sheltered spot on the far side of the chuck wagon, well away from the others, but close enough to be at the ready if there should be trouble.

"Nah." Eden brushed his offer away as she pulled off her boots, shrugged out of her jacket, unbuckled her gun belt and set it at the head of her bedroll, then lay down to wrap herself in her blanket. "Let them think what they want. I don't give a hoot."

"Me neither."

Luke kicked off his boots and pulled off his shirt, leaving him in nothing but his trousers. He had set his bedroll on the ground beside Eden's, but as soon as he lay down and drew the blanket over him, he reached for Eden.

"What in heaven's name are you doing?" she giggled

as he scooped her around, upending her entire bedroll as he jumbled hers together with his.

"Making a better bedroll," he answered.

It took a little shimmying, some sitting up and shifting around, and a lot of giggling, but within a few minutes, they'd folded the padding of their bedrolls together and thrown both thin blankets over top of both of them. Eden snuggled against Luke's side, resting her head on his shoulder and wishing more than anything that there weren't half a dozen other men within earshot. She was jumpier than a sack-full of frogs and wanted nothing more than to shed her clothes and play hide the snake with her husband. Judging by the way his body heated, he was feeling the same way.

"This was a terrible idea, you realize," she whispered, careful to be quiet enough that the others—still chatting and singing by the campfire—wouldn't hear them.

"Are you kidding? This is the best idea ever," Luke hummed back. "I've got everything right where I want it."

He proved his point by tugging her blouse out of the waist of her split skirt and sliding a hand up to squeeze her breast.

"And you expect to sleep like this?" she hissed.

"No, ma'am," he answered with a low chuckle that sent vibrations through both of them.

"Then what are we here for?"

He rolled partially over her, enough to tug her close and plant a kiss on her lips. Eden would have given into it fully, if not for the continued singing behind them.

"We're here to keep each other safe, remember?" Luke murmured breathlessly. His fingers rubbed her nipple to a hard point.

A deep, delicious ache formed in Eden's core. Her dear, sweet husband was going to drive her crazy with wanting, and there wasn't a damn thing she could do to stop them both from acute frustration. But two could play at that game.

"Sweetie," she drawled, moving a hand down his bare torso to the top of his trousers. "You asked for it."

With deft fingers, she opened the front of his trousers, tugged loose the drawstring of his drawers, and slipped her hand inside. He gasped as she stroked against his swiftly-hardening length, then tried to swallow a hungry groan.

"Shh," she scolded him, fighting not to laugh. "You want your buddies to hear you?"

"Cruel woman," he choked out.

She answered by tightening her grip, reaching down to fondle his balls before sliding her hand deftly up his length. Luke bit back an exclamation of some sort that turned into a strangled, pleading hum. Good. It served him right. She intensified her stroking, fiddling with his flared head and grinning at the slickness that came to the tip.

She was certain of her impending victory in their bedroll games when he pinched her nipple—eliciting a gasp—then burrowed his hand down along her stomach and under the waist of her skirt. She hadn't even realized he'd unhooked the back with the hand under her until his fingers sought out the curls between her legs. Her rebellious body arched toward his touch, and before she could stop herself, she'd cheated her legs apart enough for him to delve far enough to reach his goal.

"Stop," she gasped, then giggled, as he flicked at the aching nub of her pleasure.

"You stop first," he half-laughed, half-panted.

She replied by fisting him harder. He grunted, then retaliated by inching a finger closer to her entrance. He didn't have enough room to slip inside of her, but that hardly mattered. His naughty fingers slid back to tease her clitoris. The last thing Eden thought before her body burst into waves of shimmering pleasure was that she had taught him how a woman's body worked, and what she liked, a little too well on their wedding night.

She barely swallowed her cry of release as it came over her, but at least she was rewarded by Luke's groin tightening, his own muffled cry, and a slick, hot wetness that spilled over her hand. The contest left the two of them hot and panting. As the intensity of her pleasure drifted away to warm, floating completeness, Eden giggled. She kept her hand curled loosely around his softening member as Luke laughed with her.

"Uh, let's not move the blankets any time soon," he managed to whisper as the two of them snuggled closer. "I don't think it would be seemly."

Eden snorted with laughter. "No, husband, it wouldn't."

Off to the side, the singing and talking continued, which only made Eden giggle harder. Dire peril and all, she couldn't ever remember being happier.

Those warm, cuddly feelings carried her off to sleep and lasted clear until morning…when she was awaken by the sound of a revolver being cocked beside her head.

Chapter Nine

Eden gasped, scrambling in the tangle of blankets and Luke for one of her revolvers.

"Looking for this?"

Her eyes snapped up to find her brother, Braden, his Colt pointed at her with one hand, his other hand holding her gun belt. Luke's reaction was a second too slow. He thrashed in confusion at Eden's sudden movement, and as soon as his sleep-bleary eyes settled on Braden, he jolted to full wakefulness. Somehow he managed to shoot to his feet and to take Eden with him, shielding her with his body.

"Well, well, little sis," Braden snorted. He scanned the two of them—both disheveled and half-dressed, but with all the important bits covered, thank heavens. "Who's this piece of steak I found you wrapped around?"

"I'm her husband," Luke growled, the muscles of his back rippling with tension. "Who are you?"

Eden tried to scoot to the side and step around Luke, but he held her back. Of all the times for him to be a noble, protective husband.

Braden laughed, low and sour. "What, you mean she

didn't tell you about me?" His eyes widened, then narrowed to a sharp scowl. "Husband?"

It wasn't going to be good no matter how she answered. Across the way, the rest of the ranch hands were only beginning to wake up in the early morning mist. They wouldn't have a chance to reach for weapons before Braden took two or three of them out. She knew her brother too well.

"That's right," she said, trying to buy them as much time as possible. "Luke and I are married."

Braden sneered. "Now, Bitsy, what'd you go a do a fool thing like getting married for?"

Eden cringed at the name. Dread seeped through her alarm. This time, when she stepped away from Luke, he let her go.

"Bitsy?" Luke blinked at her.

"Bitsy Briscoe," Braden said. He twitched and sniffed. "She's my sister."

Luke's shoulders bunched tighter, and he pivoted to face both Eden and Braden, hands held ready at his sides. "Your sister. *Bitsy?*"

Eden licked her lips, shifting her weight from one foot to the other, wishing that she had at least one of her Peacemakers in her hands. At least she'd mentioned to Luke that she had brothers. The name thing...well, that was a problem.

She shifted to deal with Braden first. "Don't call me that." It took every nerve she had to relax her posture and face her brother's loaded gun as if it was candy floss.

Braden curled his lip at her. "What, Bitsy? It's your name."

"Not anymore."

"Eden isn't your real name?" Luke shook his head, lost.

Eden puffed out a breath. "Eden Gardner? Garden of Eden? You really didn't figure that name was made up?"

"But…" Luke's jaw hung open as his thought drifted off. He snapped it shut, shook his head, and said, "Are we really married then?"

"Yes." She swallowed. At least, they were until he figured out he should be furious with her and kicked her out of his life. That thought was so painful that she rushed on to drown it out. "I had my name legally changed after entering Hurst Home. A couple of the girls did." She turned to Braden. "I am *not* Bitsy Briscoe anymore."

It was Braden's turn to gape and shake his head. Thank God above that he lowered his guns as he did. "Brent isn't gonna like that."

The very mention of Brent's name left Eden shaking with fear. She hated every ounce of that fear, which only made her furious. "Why are you here, Braden? What do you want?"

"I'm here to fetch you," Braden said.

"But how…how did you all find me?"

Braden shrugged. "Kyle Cooter thought he saw you in Nashville. Brent sent cousin Buford to investigate. He tracked you down to some home for women. Didn't take much to corner one of those gals in an alley and make her squeal about where you'd gone next."

Eden's flash of fury over one of her friends being intimidated or worse was cut off when Braden tossed her gun belt at her feet and gestured with his own gun.

"Pack your things up and come along."

Braden started to turn away, until Eden barked, "No."

He froze, turning to stare at her with narrowed eyes. "No?"

Luke stepped into action, standing between Eden and

her brother. "She said no." It would have been far more convincing if his voice wasn't unsteady with confusion.

"It's all right, Luke." She touched his arm, wanting nothing more than to hold it, to hold him tight. Luke pivoted to send her a questioning look. Eden took a breath and faced Braden. "I'm not going anywhere with you, Braden. Luke is my husband. I'm staying with him. And even if he wasn't." She paused, the words she had tried so hard to say to her brothers for so long sticking in her throat. "I...I don't want anything to do with you boys anymore."

It hurt. Even now, such simple, straightforward words—words that made perfect sense, and that anyone with half a brain would see were the right words to say— ripped her apart. The only family she had left, and she hated them.

No, she reminded herself. It was Brent she hated. Brent was the one who broke all bonds the day he pulled the trigger and shattered what was left of everything the word "family" stood for.

Braden rubbed his stubbly chin. "Brent ain't gonna like that," he growled. "He ain't gonna like that one bit."

Eden willed her racing heart to still, her hands to stop shaking, and the tears to stop flowing. "I don't care what Brent likes." She could only manage to get the words out in a whisper. "I told him I would leave and I did."

"Yep." Braden tilted his revolver to the side, fiddling with it as if he would point and shoot at any second. "And Brent said if you left, he would hunt you down like the bitch you are and put a bullet in your head, just like he did Branch."

Luke jumped into action, lunging toward Braden, hands stretched toward his throat. The only thing that saved him from a bullet in the gut was that he caught

Braden unawares. The shock of being attacked caused Braden to stumble back and drop his gun. It was already cocked and went off. The bullet whizzed off into nothing, but the bang shook the horses and cattle nearby, and woke the rest of the camp up in a hurry.

Within seconds, Travis, Mason, and the others were up and scrambling toward the confrontation. Only a few had guns of their own, the others grabbed whatever was near to hand. Cody ended up with a frying pan. Lawson ended up with her Winchester.

"Get back," Travis shouted, leveling his revolver at Braden.

It was a pointless order. Luke already had Braden in a choke hold, fist raised.

"Stop!" Eden shouted. "Let him go."

"Let him go?" Luke echoed, incredulous. "He was going to hurt you."

"He wouldn't hurt me, he's my brother," Eden insisted, hoping she was right. "Let him go."

Luke hesitated, the tendons in his wrist tight as he squeezed Braden's neck. Braden was quickly turning purple, eyes bulging with anger more than fear. Those eyes were trained on Eden.

Mike and Billy rushed up to them. Billy dove to retrieve Braden's gun. As soon as Luke saw that there was no way Braden could get his hands on a weapon and that he had back-up, he let go.

"If you ever come anywhere near my wife again, I will hang you from the highest tree and cut your heart out." Luke's voice was so full of fury that it shook. In spite of everything, Eden's heart swelled with pride in him.

A second later, she crashed back to earth.

"You don't just walk away from the Briscoe Boys,"

Braden snarled, hoarse. He pointed a long finger at her. "You're one of us, and you always will be."

"No." Eden shook her head, throat clogged with tears. "I don't want that life anymore. I'm done with the thieving and the violence, done with it."

"Never."

"You go back and tell Brent." She summoned her last ounce of courage and added, "If you dare face him."

Braden blanched. Pure terror lit his expression as he realized what returning to Brent empty-handed would mean. Eden knew the feeling all too well.

A second later, and his face hardened with disgust. "Fine, then. Call yourself by a fancy new name and shack up with this hunk of meat as a husband. You won't live long enough to enjoy it once Brent finds out, and you know it."

Luke jerked toward him, fist upraised, but Braden learned quickly. He turned tail and sprinted for the horse that Eden now noticed standing several yards off.

"We're coming for you," he said, and with an ease that she too had practiced in years of robbing banks and trains, Braden leapt onto his mount and kicked it into a full gallop before Luke or the other ranch hands could start to move.

As soon as she was sure he was gone, Eden went limp with misery and burst into a sob. It was messy and undignified and made her feel like the worst sort of ninny, but she couldn't help it. Especially when Luke wrapped his arms around her and squeezed her tight.

"I'm sorry," she managed along with a wet sniffle after a few seconds. "I've been trying to work out a way to tell you about them. I hoped they'd leave me be, let me start over. I…I guess I knew they wouldn't." She collapsed into a fit of tears as the truth hit her.

Silence broken only by the lowing of a restless herd followed. With her face buried against Luke's chest, she couldn't see the reactions of the others, but then, she wasn't sure she wanted to see them.

"Bitsy?" Luke asked at last.

Eden winced and pushed herself far enough away from the comfort of his chest to drag her guilty eyes up to him. "I always hated that name."

"Short for Elizabeth?"

She shook her head. "Miserable father who was so upset he had an itsy, bitsy girl instead of another boy that he cursed me with it."

A hint of a smile pulled at the corners of Luke's mouth and lit his eyes. It hardened a moment later, as did his arms around her. "I'm not going to let them hurt you or take you away, but you have to tell me what's going on."

Eden swallowed and nodded. She knew it without him telling her. That gave her courage. She pushed away from him, squared her shoulders, and met his eyes.

"My name used to be Bitsy Briscoe. I was part of a gang with my brothers, the Briscoe Boys."

"The Briscoe Boys?" Lawson frowned and scratched his head. "Where have I heard that name before?"

Luke furrowed his brow. A moment later, it popped up in surprise. "I know. I heard Alice Flint and Emma Meyers talking about a gang from Missouri called the Briscoe Boys once. Seems they had a friend on their journey out West on the Oregon Trail named Lynne. Her pa was a judge from St. Louis who sentenced some members of that gang to hang. They threatened to hurt Lynne, so she went to Denver, to her uncle. She married the man who her uncle sent to escort her, Cade Lawson.

But one of the Briscoe Boys came along on the trail in disguise and tried to kill her."

Eden sighed and nodded. "That was my Uncle Ben. One of the men who was hanged was my father."

Luke and the rest of the boys stared at her with varying degrees of shock and suspicion. There was a whole lot more she needed to say. Silly though it was, she crossed to Lawson to retrieve her Winchester. Holding it, wrapping her hands around the smooth, worn wood would give her courage.

"My father and his brothers formed the original gang," she explained, fiddling with her rifle so that she didn't have to meet anyone's eyes. "That judge pretty much destroyed the gang. But at the time, my brother Brent was old enough to pick up where Pa and my uncles left off. The rest of us were just kids, though. Ma never had much of a backbone, and she was terrified of Brent. We all were."

She swallowed, choking on the memories she had of her mother. Old anger—that her mother had done nothing to protect her, that she'd let everything fall apart and only cowered in the corner while Brent bullied the rest of them—welled up in her.

"Come over here and sit down," Travis suggested.

The others hummed and nodded and jumped into action. Luke stepped up to Eden's side, slipping a hand around her waist and guiding her to the embers of the campfire that had been lit the night before. Cody and Billy rushed to find blankets for Eden to sit on, and Mason started a new fire while Lawson grabbed beans and a grinder to make coffee. Travis, Oscar, and Mike sat with her, looking ready to hang on her every word. Their kindness and show of support nearly had Eden in tears again.

As they gathered, Luke planted himself so close to her side that she was almost sitting in his lap. Eden continued to hold her Winchester with a tight grip.

"Go on," Luke said softly. "Tell us the rest."

Eden sent him a weak smile before sinking back into her memories. "Brent was revenge-minded from day one. I've never known anyone so full of hate. He taught us all how to shoot, how to ride, how to pick pockets and cheat at cards. Some of my brothers, like Braden and to a certain degree Bert, took to those evil ways like ducks to water. My youngest brother, Branch, and I only went along because if we didn't, we'd get a beating."

Luke tensed beside her, his arm holding her tight.

She shook her head and brushed that part of her past away. "I focused on what I liked best—shooting—and tried to pretend the rest didn't exist."

"You're a good shot," Lawson said, grinding coffee beans across the restarted fire.

"Yeah, we saw that," Mike agreed.

Eden shrugged, her energy drained. "As long as I kept practicing and stayed good at it, Brent didn't pay me any mind. When we all got old enough to pull a heist, he set me up as the sharpshooter. My job was to climb up to a roof near whatever bank the boys were robbing or to take cover nearby and to pick off any lawmen or anyone else who tried to come after them."

Luke drew in a breath. Several of the others' eyes grew wide with shock.

"You...you ever kill anybody?" Oscar asked what they all must be thinking.

Eden swallowed and shook her head. "I aimed for arms and legs. I never wanted to kill a soul in my life, and as God is my witness, I did everything I could not to. But I don't know what happened to the men I shot once we rode out. We never stuck around after doing a job, we always ran."

"Which is why you're so adept out here on the drive," Luke finished with an understanding nod.

"I've roughed it before," Eden confirmed. "In fact, my entire life since I was thirteen has been roughing it, more or less."

"That's why you said you just want a house and a husband and children," Luke said, letting out a long breath. He pulled her closer, planting a kiss on her head.

It was such a relief to have him understand—to have someone finally understand what her heart had longed for all these years—that it gave her the strength to get through the next part of her story.

"I left after Brent killed Branch."

The camp went still, all eyes on her with a mixture of horror and pity. No one said a word, so she went on.

"We'd just robbed a train in eastern Kansas. That's as far out West as we'd ever gone before. By that point, Branch and I were through. The robbery was messy, Braden broke his arm and Bert got shot. So did Branch, but it was only a graze. He'd had it, though. That night, Branch put his foot down. He said he was through, that he wanted to go clean and start a new life. Brent argued and threatened, said there was no better life. It got bad."

Her voice failed on the last words. Her heart bled with sorrow and regret. Tears stung her eyes.

"I loved Branch," she went on in a half sob. "He was the only good thing in my life. He was my brother, my true brother, heart and soul. But when Brent raised that gun and pointed it at his head, I froze. I didn't do anything to stop him or protect Branch. I didn't...I didn't think he'd actually do it. But he did."

She flinched at the memory of Brent's gun firing,

Branch jerking and twisting as the life snapped out of him. Now as it was then, she went numb, stomach churning.

Luke pulled her onto his lap and hugged her so hard the black memories flew away. He buried his face in her hair and whispered, "I'm so sorry."

Eden was sorely tempted to disappear into the comfort of his embrace, but the story wasn't over.

"I did nothing," she whispered. "I stood by and let Brent shoot him. We all just sort of locked up and stared at Branch's body on the floor afterwards. Even Braden and Bert were horrified. Brent didn't have a lick of remorse, though. He spit on Branch's body and said that that's what any of us would get if we ever crossed him." She took a deep breath and went on with, "I left that night when they were all asleep."

"Good," Cody exclaimed with a fierce nod.

"And you went to Hurst Home?" Mason asked.

Eden shrugged. "Eventually. I didn't know where I was going and I only had so much money. I zigzagged back from Kansas, but I knew I couldn't go home to St. Louis. I drifted south, trying to stay away from big cities, until I figured out that there were more people in big cities and I could hide better. I ran into a traveling preacher and his wife in Memphis, and they told me about Hurst Home. I've never been more surprised in my life than when Mrs. Breashears took me in with no questions asked."

"And thank the Lord she did," Luke said, holding her as if he would never let go.

Eden did thank Him. Every damn day. Her story was over, so she let out the tension she'd been holding and sank into the warmth and protection of her husband's embrace.

Her relief was short-lived, though.

With a wince, she said, "Braden wasn't lying or

making stuff up to scare us. Brent won't be happy, and he *will* come after me."

"He can try," Cody growled from his seat across the campfire, hands balled to fists.

"Yeah," Billy agreed. "If he shows his rotten face, we'll bring him to justice."

Eden's heart swelled at the support, but it burned and ached all the same. She shook her head. "You don't understand. Brent is a cold-blooded killer. Braden and Bert aren't much better. Who knows who else Brent has with him. We have plenty of cousins who are just as mean and bent on reviving the Briscoe gang, and any number of them could be with Brent. I know it's him following us because of the spyglass."

"Spyglass?" Cody asked.

"Brent once stole this gold spyglass from a shop in St. Louis. It's for ships at sea, to help captains see far distances. He uses it to scout out banks and trains."

"And to see into cattle drives from long distances," Luke finished her thought. His voice was deadly calm, like he was plotting how to take the entire Briscoe gang down.

Eden twisted in his arms to face him. "However many of them there are out there, they're deadly, Luke. They've killed men without batting an eyelash. It's what they do." She twisted back to the others. "You're all brave and kind and strong, but you're ranch hands, not killers."

"It doesn't matter," Mason said, standing. "We brought weapons. We'll protect you."

A chorus of agreement rose up from the others. They stood as well, searching for whatever weapons they'd brought with them. Eden was bolstered by the show, but at the same time her heart broke.

"Could you really kill a man?" she asked them.

"If they threatened you, yes," Luke answered. "I'd kill them with my bare hands."

Tears stung her eyes, but still she smiled. "Thank you."

"We've still got the herd to worry about," Travis said, jumping into action. "The stockyard isn't that far, from what I know. We need to keep moving forward either way."

The others hummed in agreement.

"Can we get the cattle to a safe spot, maybe a defensible area, and wait for the Briscoe Boys?" Lawson asked.

"Looks like we'll have to," Travis said. "What we need is a hill of some sort."

Travis went on, plotting where they should go and how they could set up a defensible position to protect Eden and the cattle at the same time. Eden tried to listen, but the weight of her past pressed her down. She closed her eyes and hid her face against Luke's shoulder.

"Hey," he whispered, rubbing her back. "It'll be all right."

"Are you sure?" she muttered.

"Sure as I've ever been. I may not have ever killed a man, but I've been in fights before." His sudden laugh brought her head up. "Who would've thought that the same skills that got me in trouble half a dozen times would help me out now?"

Eden relaxed into a smile. She rested a shaky hand against the side of his face. "Taking a chance and coming out here to marry you is the best thing that ever happened to me."

His grin filled with pride and passion. "Honey, Chance is my name. Of course you would take a chance on me."

She shook her head at his ability to joke in such dire circumstances. But then, that's what made her heart sing when she looked at him. She leaned closer, bringing her lips to his. He answered by kissing her with a force of passion that said more than mere words ever could. He would protect and defend her for the rest of her days, like no one ever had before.

"Right," he said with a rumbling confidence as their kiss ended. "Let's get moving. We've got a fight to plan."

Chapter Ten

Every struggle for recognition and respect that Luke had ever fought through, every bitter, grumbling thought when he wasn't taken seriously or when jokes were made about him, vanished. He sat astride Marshall—a rifle slanted across the saddle in front of him, Eden only a few yards to his left—with his jaw set. In that moment, he didn't give two figs what anyone thought of him. His wife was in danger, and he would protect her.

"They still there?" Billy called from behind him in drag position.

Luke and Eden both twisted in their saddles to look past the dust kicked up by the herd at the same time as Oscar did to search the horizon behind them. They'd been moving the herd forward as fast as they dared since right after breakfast. The whole lot of them had silently agreed that their best course of action was to get Eden as far away from her brothers as they could before finding a defensible position to stand and fight. Luke wanted her to ride in the chuck wagon with Mike, but she wasn't having any of that.

The first rider had appeared behind them barely fifteen minutes after they had moved out. Two more had joined the first within an hour. Now, as Luke squinted at the horizon, there were at least six of them. Brothers and cousins, if Eden was right. Ruthless, practiced thugs.

Luke tightened his hand on the rifle. "They're still plenty far behind us."

He glanced across to Eden, who had her Winchester loaded and ready and her revolvers only a breath away at her belt. As much as it had ripped Luke up to see her crying and afraid as she told the heartbreaking story of her life, it filled him with pride now to see her so determined. She didn't smile when their eyes met, but she did nod with all the confidence of a woman who would rather die than return to the hell of her past.

Ahead of them, Travis and Lawson were riding at point. Luke was too far away to make out what they were saying to each other over the steady thunder of the herd, but he could tell by the expressions they both wore that they were worried. Of all the times for the land they traveled across to be flat and barren as far as the eye could see, this was the worst. They needed a hill. They needed a stream, trees, anything that could provide cover and keep the cattle out of the way.

"How much money will Mr. Haskell lose if the cattle don't make it to the stockyard?" Eden asked, sensing the problem that only added to their worries.

"More than I'm worth," Luke replied, scanning the tense herd.

"Aw, come on, Luke. You're worth far more than that to me."

Her reply was stilted and her smile didn't hold, but the very fact that she had tried to make a joke stuck like a bone in Luke's throat.

"Eden Chance, you are far and away the bravest woman I've ever met," he told her, loud and sure.

Her cheeks flushed pink, and this time her smile held. "Does it still count as bravery if you have no damn choice?"

"Hell, yes." Luke winked at her. "In fact, I think it counts double *because* you have no choice."

Her smile turned watery. "I can't believe that I've known you for less than a week, but already I don't know what I'd do without you."

And that was another thing he was coming to learn about women, about this woman in particular. She could say the most beautiful things and still have them cut him like a knife.

"Sweetheart, next summer, you and I are gonna sit on the porch of our new house, rocking our baby and laughing about how we drove cattle and escaped crazy Uncle Brent on our honeymoon."

Eden made a noise somewhere between a laugh and a sob. "Let's not confuse the little 'uns by calling him 'Uncle Brent,' okay?"

Luke shook his head, his expression turning deadly. "Well it's not appropriate to call him what I'd like to call him around children."

Eden huffed with unsteady laughter, then brushed at her face, blinking. Even though he knew better, Luke chose to tell himself she just had dust in her eyes. She was far too heroic for anything else.

"Luke!" The call came from Travis at the front of the herd. "Get up here!"

Luke waved at Travis, then turned to Eden. "You okay here on your own for a bit?"

"Yeah," she answered with a nod.

Luke twisted in his saddle to gesture to Oscar

anyhow. As Oscar adjusted his position from drag to somewhere between the back and the right flank, Luke kicked Marshall to a run up to the front of the herd. "What's going on?"

Travis sighed and rubbed his dirty face. None of them had had time to wash up, and with the dust from the herd, they looked like vagabonds. "I don't see any hills," he said.

"Nope." There was no sense beating around the bush when there weren't any bushes either.

"What I do see is half a dozen men closing in on is from behind."

Luke clenched his jaw and tightened his grip on his rifle and his reins. "Yep."

Travis paused before going on with, "We've got to do something."

"I agree, but what?" Luke asked.

It was impossible to stop and confer with the size of the herd and the way they plodded on. Even the cattle sensed that something was wrong. Rather than walk steadily, their eyes were wide and they lowed more than usual. They'd been gathering in strays from the edges of the herd all day. Now that the sun was high in the sky, they were hot and tired to boot.

"I don't know," Travis admitted. "We can't be far from the stockyard, but I don't see any sign of a town or civilization nearby."

"We're out in the middle of nowhere, that's for sure," Lawson added.

Knowing they were right didn't help the situation. Luke glanced over his shoulder as much as he could while his horse kept moving. Eden had gone to chase after three cows that had veered to the right. Over on the other side, Mason and Cody had their hands full keeping the left flank from wandering off. They were all working too hard just to keep the herd in line, let alone to formulate a plan to take on the Briscoe Boys. Luke could still make them out beyond the cloud of dust lingering behind the herd. Worse still, they looked to be closer.

"We can't just skip along and wait for them to catch up to us," Luke said, half thinking aloud. "We need to be the ones who take this fight to them. For Eden's sake."

"I agree," Travis said. "But how?"

Luke rubbed the dirt and sweat off his face and looked around at what they had. Not much. A couple hundred cattle and a whole mess of open land. They were out in the open, exposed. He'd be a fool to think that Eden was the only one of the Briscoes who was a good shot. All her brothers needed to do was get close enough to fire a rifle, and they'd be in trouble.

As if someone back there could hear his thoughts, a blast of smoke appeared near one of the pursuing riders. A moment later, a whizzing thud hit the dirt behind some of the cattle near the back of the herd on the left. A few bellowed and made a break for it.

"To the right, the right!" Travis called as Billy raced forward and Mason hung back to gather the terrified beasts in. They managed to steer the cows back into the herd, but the entire bunch of cattle on the left flank was now agitated.

"The last thing we need now is a stampede," Travis grumbled.

Luke scowled at the thought. His heart pounded at the very thought of trying to control a rampaging mess of cattle while also evading a pack of killers. It would be complete chaos. The noise and the dust alone would—

As the idea hit him, Luke's jaw dropped open. He blinked as he twisted the other way in his saddle to check on Eden. She was moving smoothly to the side of the right flank. Oscar was shadowing her. Farther behind, her brothers were closing the gap, slowly but surely.

"Stampede." Luke nudged Marshall to take him closer to Travis. "We need a stampede."

"Are you nuts?" Travis growled. "The herd would scatter. It would be madness. There wouldn't be enough of us to—" He stopped, and his eyes went round.

Luke nodded. "Scare the cattle and get them running every which way. The faster the better. We start them running in a circle, move them to the right. We'll keep Eden on the other side, in the middle if we have to."

Travis shook his head. "She could be trampled."

"She knows how to ride. She could keep out of their way. The cattle will act as a shield, stopping her brothers from getting to her," Luke continued with his plan.

"They can still shoot at her," Lawson worried.

"They can try, but they'll have the rest of us charging right at them."

"Not to mention a herd of terrified cattle," Travis finished the thought.

"They might have the advantage when it comes to willingness to kill," Luke went on, "but I'm willing to bet they've never faced a stampede. We have. All of us but Eden know how to handle that kind of mess, and so do our horses."

"Their horses will panic." Lawson's face lit up. "Let's do it."

Luke glanced to Travis. Eden was his and the idea was his, but for all intents and purposes, the cattle were Travis's. A real leader knew when to rely on the strengths of others.

"We'll need an insane amount of luck for this to

work," Travis said, but already Luke could see the flash of decision in his eyes.

"We'll make our own luck." Luke nodded.

The plan was set. Travis nodded and sent Lawson off to the left to let Mason and Cody know. Luke adjusted his hat to sit tight on his head, then turned and circled around to ride back to Eden's side. Behind them, the Briscoe Boys were closer still, so close Luke was beginning to be able to tell them apart. He gestured for Oscar to ride up and join them.

"We haven't got much time," he said, fast and serious. "We're going to start a stampede. Turn them to the right, confuse the Briscoes. Eden, stay behind the herd or inside of the circle once they start to run themselves out."

"But I can fight," she said. "I've got my guns."

And Luke didn't believe for a moment that she would use them against her own brothers, no matter how evil they were. "Can you shoot from the saddle? Over a distance?"

"Yeah," she admitted.

"Then do what you do best. Pick them off from a distance, and let us go in close."

Panic stretched the lines of her face. "Luke, if you end up in danger, if you get hurt—"

"Then I know you've got my back," he finished. "You've always got my back."

Her lips worked, pursing and opening like she had more to say, but she kept it to herself. At last, she nodded.

"What if we—"

Oscar's question was snapped off as one of the Briscoes fired another shot at the herd. It ricocheted off the ground and bit into one of the cattle's backsides. The injured animal let out a horrific cry and bolted forward.

All of the cows around it panicked and burst into action as well. Oscar cursed under his breath, but Luke grinned with fatal humor.

"Nice of them to get things started for us," he growled, ready to fight. "Let's go!"

If the constant walking of the cattle that Eden has listened to for the last few days was like rumbling around her, the moment the herd broke into a run, stampeding, it was like thunder every way she turned. It was only right. Every time she'd looked over her shoulder for the last hour—making out first Braden and Bert's faces, then Brent himself, then several of her cousins—she had felt the approaching storm. That didn't prepare her for the terror of over two hundred cattle rampaging.

"Get around them!" Luke shouted. He waved and pointed to both her and Oscar.

She hesitated for only a second before kicking her horse to a run through the swirling cloud of dust in back of the charging herd. One minute the bulk of the herd had been right beside her, the next it was almost completely in front of her. She didn't have time to yank up the scarf around her neck to cover her face and ended up tasting dirt, breathing it in.

There wasn't time to be distracted by coughing either. Shots fired from the back of the cloud, and by the time she made it through and twisted to get her bearings, the Briscoe Boys had launched into a full gallop, guns blazing. She recognized Bert's whooping cry, Brent's wordless shouts. Her blood ran cold, but the ice turned to steel in her veins.

Gripping her Winchester for all she was worth, she tugged on her reins to turn her horse toward the front of the stampede. Luke had told her to get in front of it, to use the herd as a shield once they were able to get the cattle to turn and circle around. Frustrating though it was, her life had been saved by doing exactly what Brent said more times than she wanted to count. It was better to listen to Luke than to go rogue.

She questioned that thought almost as soon as she had it. As more gunshots fired—some from ahead of her now—confusion rose up to choke her more than dust. Everything was a blur of movement. The thick, black and brown bodies of the cows blended with clouds of dust. She couldn't make out who was riding or even what direction they were riding in as her friends zipped past her, hollering. All she could do was point her horse forward, keeping the speeding chuck wagon in sight as a guide, and hope it knew where to take her.

"Eden, this way!"

Luke's shout snapped her out of growing panic. She risked sticking her head up to find him. He rode far to the side, shouting and waving his arms at the cattle. When had they ridden so far in front of the herd?

It didn't matter. Through the confusion, she could see Travis and Lawson up ahead, shouting and gesturing like wild men. It made no sense. Then again, the lead cattle were beginning to veer to the right.

Purpose caught hold in Eden's brain once more, and she urged her horse to gallop on to the back of the growing curve. She sailed past Luke, and then Mason, who pulled their mounts up and charged for the back of the stampede. There was so much noise that Eden couldn't make out what was the thunder of cattle and what was gunshot and shouting. All she knew was that she had to get in back of the herd.

By the time she galloped past Travis, the majority of the cattle at the back had arced into a huge curve. She could just make out Lawson—on the far side of that curve now—urging the beasts to run in a circle. They followed his direction—miraculously—turning and turning in on themselves until the force of so much forward motion swerved in on itself in a spiral. Eden gasped as the cattle in the center of the circle ground to a stop, standing and lowing as if nothing were out of the ordinary.

She only had a heartbeat to marvel at the speed with which the stampeding cattle calmed themselves. Shots rang out from the vast, torn up plain they had just galloped across. She tugged her mount to a stop and lifted in her saddle, pushing her hat off so that she could see more clearly. About a quarter of the herd had dashed off in a dozen different directions and now dotted the landscape as they continued to run. The men on horseback, however, were converging in a spot fifty yards behind the bulk of the herd.

Shots rang out. Smoke rose up from rifles on both sides. Eden wiped her face with the back of her sleeve, panting and coughing as she scanned the unfolding scene. Brent rode in the center, behind the others. Braden charged ahead, firing as his horse galloped. Fool. His aim was terrible when he tried that trick. She swallowed at the thought. All the better. Bert hung back by Brent's side. Her cousins fanned out, slowing their horses to a stop and firing.

Eden was almost ready to sit steady in her saddle to wait things out when a cry split the air and Mason fell from his saddle.

"No!" Cody shouted. He jerked his horse around and charged toward his brother. Eden didn't hear the gunshot, but she saw him jerk as he too was hit. Billy and Luke saw and shouted with enough ferocity that Eden felt it across the distance.

Without hesitation, Eden raised her Winchester and took aim. "Arms, legs, miss the horse." Her old mantra echoed in her head as she let out a breath, squinted down the barrel of her rifle, and fired at one of her cousins, Blane. The crack and jolt of the shot, the smoke and the spent cartridge flying was so familiar it calmed her. Blane jerked to the side, dropping his rifle as he clapped a hand on his arm, twisting and falling off his horse.

"One," she said, voice little more than a croak, and stood in her stirrups.

She swung her rifle around, aiming at another cousin, her Uncle Bo's oldest, Butch. Her muscles tensed, she held her breath. "Arms, legs, miss the horse." Again her rifle banged as the shot released. Butch lurched to the side, clawing at his thigh and spilling from his horse.

Like lightning, Eden picked out another cousin, Ted, the black sheep. Her courage faltered and she let out a whimper. Ted used to say he wanted to be a schoolteacher, that the only person who had ever treated him nice was the wizened old booby who they'd made fun of every day back in their one-room schoolhouse in Missouri. Ted had been sweet on a girl who had tried over and over to be Eden's friend. She'd been too scared to accept that friendship, and eventually the girl moved out West with her family. The flood of memories hit her in the blink of an eye. Ted hadn't wanted this any more than she had. She couldn't shoot him, she couldn't shoot him, she couldn't—

A crack sounded, and Ted tumbled off his horse. Eden screamed. Frantically, she searched for which of her new friends had shot him. But no, Billy was too far away, Mason and Cody were on the ground. Oscar was close to Ted, but he was turned in the wrong direction. In the wrong direction?

She clenched her jaw, whipping to pick Brent out of the mass of confusion. Her brother had just pulled his revolver up, as if he'd fired a shot. He was looking straight at Ted. Ted must have hesitated, not killed Oscar when he could. A surge of pride in her cousin filled Eden.

It died a heartbeat later as Brent shifted to face Luke and fired without a second thought. Luke jerked to the side.

"No!"

Orders be damned. Eden kicked her horse into a flat run, darting straight toward the heart of the conflict, straight toward Brent. Even the stray, confused cattle that wandered into her path couldn't stop her from charging. If Luke was hurt—or worse—she wouldn't be responsible for what she did.

"Brent," she cried out as she drew close to the heart of the conflict.

Butch and Blane rolled in the dirt, clutching the limbs that Eden had shot. Ted lay face up not far to the side, grimacing in pain. Eden thanked God that he wasn't dead. Mason lay motionless several yards beyond, Cody crouched over him, blocking Eden's view. She couldn't tell if he was dead or not. Braden and Bert continued to shoot at Oscar, Billy, and now Travis, who had galloped up to the scene on her heels. Was he protecting her?

She didn't have time to wonder. Luke had righted himself in his saddle, though dark red stained his left sleeve. Brent raised his revolver to fire at him again. The shot missed, but Eden screamed anyhow.

"Eden, get back!" Luke ordered.

He took his eyes off of Brent. With a sneer, Brent took aim a third time.

Eden pulled her horse to a stop and raised her rifle.

"Arms, legs, miss the horse," she whispered, took aim, and fired.

Brent dodged to the side, deliberately or by luck it was hard to tell. It didn't matter; his attention veered away from Luke and landed straight on her.

"Bitsy Briscoe," he shouted.

Oscar and Billy stopped fighting and whipped toward her. Braden and Bert lowered their weapons. The whole, chaotic scene went still.

"Bitsy Briscoe," Brent repeated. "Who the hell do you think you are?"

Eden gasped for breath, her Winchester still raised and pointed at her brother. She could fire, but she had a bad feeling she'd shot the last bullet in her rifle's magazine. Her arms shook too hard for her to get a good shot off anyhow.

Luke wheeled his horse around and drew a revolver from his belt. He aimed and cocked it at Brent, fury scarring his dirty face. A half second later, Braden and Bert's guns clicked to ready. More snaps and clicks followed as everyone raised and pointed their weapons.

"No," Eden shouted. "This is between me and my brother."

Confused glances snapped to her from both sides. She did her best to ignore them. Her attention was focused completely on Brent, on his wicked sneer, his grubby face—a face that could have been handsome, if it wasn't filled with so much hate. Even when he looked at her, his kin.

"Itsy Bitsy," he laughed, the sound a sick grumble. He shook his head. "What do you think you're doing? Don't you know, sweet little sister, that no one walks away from me?"

"I told you then and I'm telling you now—I don't

want any part of this gang or this family anymore." She cursed her voice for shaking as she made her declaration.

Brent continued to chuckle as he settled into a seemingly relaxed posture on his horse. "You can't escape blood," he said, opening his arms. "You can run all you like and change your name as many times as suits you. Hell, you can marry as many dummies as you want and even pop out a few kids of your own. But you'll always be mine, my blood, my kin." He cocked his head to the side. "Come to think of it, any kids you have will be my blood too."

"No." She shook her head, Winchester still aimed in spite of her fear. "My babies will be Luke's babies. I'm his now. I never was yours."

Brent shook his head. He gestured to Luke, who tensed like a tiger, hand flexing on the handle of his gun. "See that blood on his sleeve?" Brent said. "It'll be all over the rest of him, and all I have to do is lift a hand. One of the boys will shoot your sweet husband dead before he can so much as blink. And you know why?"

Eden ignored his question. "You do and I'll shoot."

"Because they're mine too," he answered as if her threat meant nothing. "Bert?"

To Brent's side, Bert shifted his already cocked revolver to point at Luke's head.

"You wouldn't," Eden sobbed.

Bert squirmed in his saddle, eyes darting between Eden and Brent, face pinched in panic.

"Only a coward threatens women," Luke snarled, keeping his gun aimed squarely at Brent. Fury rippled off of him, but so did strength. He leaned toward Eden, unable to run to her or draw her to him. "Only a demon threatens his sister."

"Yeah?" Brent shrugged. "Only a fool crosses a Briscoe."

"Then call me a fool," Luke said, "Because I will die ten times over and take you down with me if you so much as sniff in her direction."

Brent's chuckle sent shivers down Eden's back. "You think you stand a chance against me?"

"Yep," Luke answered. "I think I stand more of a chance. Because I love this woman."

Eden gasped, her rifle lowering as her arms went weak.

"I love her like I've never loved anyone before," Luke went on. "She was brave enough to come out here and marry me without knowing a thing about me. She married a restless boy, and made me into a man. And men protect the women they love. They shelter them from harm, give them reason to wake up and try for the best every day. They keep them safe, even if it means losing their own life. So don't you go telling me that Eden is yours, because you wouldn't know the meaning of real love if it was written across the sky in flames."

Brent's smug grin melted into a deadly sneer. His hand flexed around his gun, and even though he kept it lowered, Eden knew he was ready to fire at any second. Her lips trembled as she scrambled to figure out how to tell Luke, but Luke spoke on.

"Eden tells me you shot her brother, Branch, in cold blood because he wanted out like she did."

From the ground where they were watching, Eden's cousins flinched. Braden's expression hardened to bitterness, but Bert's contorted to misery. All in the blink of an eye.

"You can threaten us all you like, but Eden has a new life, a new purpose," Luke went on. "End of story. I'll give you ten seconds to put away your guns and walk away for good, or else I'll do what I have to to make sure my wife is free of her past forever." He paused, then said in a loud voice, "One. Two. Thr—"

It happened in the blink of an eye. Just as Eden had feared, Brent raised his gun and fired. A flurry of other gunshots sounded at the same time. Eden flinched, dropping her rifle as gun smoke swirled into the air around her.

A heartbeat later, Brent curled over his horse, dropping to the ground. Braden flinched to the side, dropping as well.

Eden screamed and jerked toward Luke, but to her surprise, he still sat tall and strong atop his horse, no smoke curling up from his gun. It took her frantic mind a moment to grasp who had fired—Bert, Butch, and Ted. Braden writhed in pain in the dirt. Brent was still, a pool of blood forming under him.

Eden gaped, her stomach turning. At the same time, an odd lightness filled her chest. Free. The word repeated itself over and over in her head. Free, free, free. Her glance darted up to meet Bert's eyes, only to find the feeling reflected there. Bert's tormented grimace was gone, replaced by pale, wide-eyed shock. That shock softened to regret so deep it lined Bert's eyes with red. Eden felt tears sting at her own eyes.

"Go on and live your life...Eden," Bert all but whispered. "Go be happy."

Beyond words, all Eden could do was nod as tears drew lines through the dirt on her cheeks. She couldn't swallow the lump in her throat. But for once, it wasn't fear and sorrow choking her, it was joy—the joy of putting the darkness of her past behind her forever.

Bert turned to their cousins, still on the ground. "Can you ride?"

The three of them grunted and groaned, but pushed themselves to their feet. Now that he was up, Eden could see that Ted had been hit in his shoulder. All three of her cousins managed to limp and drag themselves to their horses. Butch hauled a still-groaning Braden up over the back of one of their horses, and Ted and Blane managed to load Brent's body over his mount.

"Wait, they shot Mason and Cody," Billy argued. "They should face the law."

He lunged forward, gun still drawn.

"No." Travis stopped him. Billy was so used to following orders from Travis that he froze in his path and turned to Travis in confusion. Travis shook his head. "If Eden says they go, then they go."

"But…but they're outlaws," Billy protested.

Her cousins had all made it to their horses. Bert gave Eden one last nod before they nudged their horses into as fast a retreat as they could manage in their beat up state. As relieved as she was to wash her hands of the Briscoe Boys forever, her heart ached for the family she'd lost. The trouble was, she'd lost them a long time ago.

"Let them go," she said with a sniffle. "They've suffered enough already, and chances are they have a lot more suffering ahead of them." It was bad enough that she had to live with the part she'd played in Brent's schemes, but the rest of the boys had killed men, hurt people. It was far harder for a man with goodness buried at his core to live with himself knowing that, living free, than to face it locked up in a cell somewhere.

She said a quick, final prayer for her kin, then turned away, squeezing her eyes shut. Bitsy Briscoe was dead for good. She opened her eyes as Eden Chance, now and forever, and looked to Luke.

Luke watched her with a mix of love and pride and sadness that filled her heart to bursting. He didn't have to say anything, she knew every good, kind word she'd ever wanted a man to say to her was in him through the force of the love in his eyes alone.

"Think we could go home and get started on those babies now?" she asked, weak, weepy, but so desperate to do just that that her heart was nearly bursting.

"Sure, sweetheart," he answered, his voice like a caress. "Anything you want."

He nudged his horse to walk closer to her, close enough that he could reach out and brush the tears away from her dirty face with his thumb. Then he leaned across to kiss her, so full of power and emotion that Eden could only close her eyes and consign her heart to him forever.

Chapter Eleven

Luke had never been so happy to ride under the iron arch welcoming folks home to Paradise Ranch as he was when he and Eden and the boys passed under it a week later.

"Who ever thought that this old place would be such a sight for sore eyes," Cody said, rubbing the bandage under his shirt where the bullet had grazed his side.

"I dunno," Lawson hummed, removing his hat to wipe his brow with his sleeve. "I always liked it. Never wanted to be anywhere else."

"It's Paradise," Eden sighed. Her smile was worn and exhausted, but few things had ever filled Luke with so much satisfaction.

Eden had been quiet after her brothers and cousins rode off, keeping her thoughts to herself as they set to work gathering the stray cows that had wandered away from the herd and fitting things back together. Mason was too injured to help, and even though Cody had been shot too, he concentrated solely on getting his brother into the chuck wagon and making sure he was as comfortable as he could be. They'd had to camp right there where the fight had taken place that night, but after a few hours of travel the next day, they made it to the stockyard in Culpepper.

Fortunately for them all, Culpepper had a doctor who knew his trade. He pulled a bullet out of Mason's leg and managed to stave off infection in the process. At least so far. Mason was still resting out in Culpepper with Oscar to keep him company until the doctor said he was out of danger. The rest of them had completed the transaction with Howard's herd, tucked into a hotel for the night, and set out to bring the horses back the next day. Without the cattle to slow them down, the journey home took far less time.

Eden had kept her eyes open, scanning the land around them and the horizon across every mile.

"You looking for them?" Luke had asked her at one point.

She replied with a nod and a wistful sigh. "Don't know if I want to find a trace of them or not."

Luke understood. He thought he understood the bittersweet way she'd cried in his arms last night when they were close enough to Paradise Ranch to know that they weren't going to find a single sign of her kin. That was it. That part of her life was truly over. Luke tried to show respect and not feel too smug over the fact that her life was now completely his.

No, she wasn't his, they were each other's.

A rider charging toward them from the path leading to Howard's house shook him out of his thoughts. "Whoa." He motioned for Eden and the others to stop so he could make out who the rider was.

His brow flew up when he saw it was Franklin Haskell. It always struck him as uncanny how nimble

Franklin was atop a horse when his legs were broken and encased in braces.

"You're back," Franklin hollered once he was within earshot. "Thank God, you're back."

Luke exchanged a confused look with Eden, then glanced past her to Travis. Travis shrugged.

"A little late, but at least we made it back in one piece, more or less," Travis answered Franklin.

Franklin pulled his horse up and slowed until he was breathless and dancing in front of them. "We received a telegram from Culpepper, from a Dr. Xavier Fellowes, a bill for his services."

Luke snorted and shook his head, a wry grin on his face. Eden chuckled along with him.

"Figures," she said. "No doctor that good was ever going to let us get away with a smile and a handshake."

"Especially when he found out who we work for," Luke agreed.

Franklin gaped at the two of them. "What's this I hear about a shoot-out? Mason is going to be fine, but are the rest of you all right? Was it Bonneville's men?" His expression darkened.

"It wasn't Bonneville," Travis said, holding up his hands.

A curious look came over Franklin. "There was another man poking around the ranch right after you left. A drifter named...named 'B' something. Did he have anything to do with—"

"It was some other gang." Luke rushed in with a sidelong glance to Eden. "Some bandits who must've thought they could rustle some of the cattle and make a quick buck."

He checked to see if she approved. Since the moment Bert and the others walked off, even though they were asked several times in Culpepper what had happened, an unspoken agreement had sprung up between them all that no one would ever mention who had attacked them or Eden's connection to them.

Eden glanced off at the horizon, eyes troubled. Her hand moved toward her Winchester, strapped to her saddle. Luke wasn't sure if she was aware of the movement or not.

"Cattle thieves," Franklin said, his frown betraying that he wasn't convinced. "And you're sure they had nothing at all to do with Rex Bonneville?"

Travis caught Luke's eye, then cleared his throat and faced Franklin. "Pretty darn sure."

"But—"

"Let's ride back to the house where we can talk about it with your father and Mrs. Piedmont too," Travis cut him off with a weary smile. "My backside sure could use a comfy chair to sit in instead of a saddle, for a change."

"Of course." Franklin's shoulders loosened and he laughed. "Sorry, I'm just so glad to see that you're all safe and whole. Really." He met each of their eyes with all the seriousness of a man who wished he'd been able to be there to help his friends.

Luke relaxed even further as they continued on to Howard's house and the barn and stable. It was good to have friends, good to have a home. He glanced to Eden as she tilted her head up to the sun, eyes closed, and let out a long sigh. It was good to have a strong, beautiful wife too.

"Land sakes, look at the lot of you." Mrs. Piedmont clapped a hand to her chest and ran down the stairs from the front porch of Howard's house as they rode their horses to their final stop in the yard beside the barn.

Luke had never been so glad to dismount in his life, and judging by the wince on Eden's sweet face, the feeling was mutual. He crossed to give her a reassuring hug, but was interrupted as Mrs. Piedmont, Josephine, and Elizabeth Haskell charged toward them.

"Oh, my sweet boy, we heard all about what happened." Josephine launched herself right at him, squeezing him so tight that Luke nearly fell over.

"It was nothing, Ma." Luke made light of it, sending Eden a wry grin. "Eden took good care of me and kept me safe."

"Oh my dear, I am so sorry that you had to endure that ordeal," Elizabeth said. In all the time Luke had known Howard's wife, she'd never been particularly demonstrative, but she folded Eden in a tight hug now, as though Eden were her daughter.

Eden's eyes went wide, and she pleaded with Luke for help over Elizabeth's slim shoulder. Luke could only chuckle. If it would help Eden to see that she belonged here, that these were her people now, he'd line all of Haskell up to give her bear-hugs.

He was still smirking at Eden's discomfort when Howard marched up to him, slapped him hard on the back, and said, "Luke, my boy! Mason telegraphed all about it! Said you were a real hero."

Luke nearly choked on the declaration. "He did?"

"Of course he did." Howard pivoted to find Travis, who was halfway through ordering Howard's stable hands to take care of the horses. "I hear Luke carried himself with admirable command during your little adventure. Is it true?"

"Yep," Travis said without hesitation. "He's a real leader, that one."

Luke's jaw dropped, even as a warm, prickly feeling of surprised happiness rose up his spine. "Well, I had help," he stuttered.

"A bit," Travis went on, "but it was Luke who took charge when those bandits tried to make off with some of the cows." He crossed toward them, thumping Luke on the back as he passed. "Sometimes you need a man who knows how to pick a fight to keep situations from getting out of hand." He winked at Luke and nodded at Eden before heading on to the bunkhouse.

Howard laughed, his whole body shaking. "That's just what I thought. Sounds like I'll need to find more challenging work for you to do around here in the future, eh? As Travis's assistant, maybe?" He elbowed Luke so hard Luke nearly fell over. Howard turned to Eden. "And look at you, Mrs. Chance."

"Me?" Through her exhaustion, Eden managed to find the humor of Howard's exuberant personality.

"Yes, you. Look at that split skirt, those revolvers in your belt, the dirt covering you from head to toe." Howard pointed from her to his wife and back again. "You're as sharp a ranch hand as any of the rest of them."

"Howard," Elizabeth scolded him. "Mrs. Chance is a lady."

Eden laughed out loud. "Now there's one thing I've never been called before." She blossomed into a smile, as if being reminded she was no pampered miss brought her back to herself. Luke's heart flipped in his chest.

"I tell you what." Howard narrowed his eyes and wagged a finger at her. "If you want a job working my ranch alongside your husband, it's yours."

"Howard!" Elizabeth hissed a second time.

"Well?" Howard shrugged. "If Virginia can do it, then Eden here can do it too. What do you say?" He turned a huge smile on Eden.

Luke was just beginning to warm to the idea of working beside his amazing wife every day when Eden laughed and shook her head. "No, thank you, sir," she said. "I came out here because I wanted to keep house and get cozy with a husband and raise a whole parcel of children, if you don't mind my saying."

Elizabeth looked relieved. Virginia smiled in approval. Howard laughed and shrugged. "It was worth a try."

"And I think you'll find that, before too long, it'll be easier to get those things done than ever," Virginia added. "The carpenters have been hard at work on your new house over in the Village. It should be done by month's end."

It was the best news Luke had heard all day.

"Now go get yourselves cleaned up, then join us in the house. It won't take Molly but a moment to put together a feast worthy of our returning heroes," Howard said.

"Well, it might take longer than that," Elizabeth muttered.

"We'll eat whatever we can find until then," Howard finished.

"No doubt you will," Elizabeth sighed.

Luke and Eden laughed together, then headed across to the Hen House to clean up.

Eden wasn't sure how she made it through the noisy, crazy supper that Howard's cook, Molly, managed to throw together for them. They had all been exhausted riding the last few miles back to the ranch, but as soon as food was served and beer poured, it was like they were given new life. Howard wanted to hear every bit of what had happened in full detail. Eden was more than happy to sit back, belly full, and let the others come up with whatever yarn they wanted to spin to keep anyone from learning the truth.

Later, when she walked across the yard in the twilight, hand-in-hand with Luke, she spared one last glance to the horizon.

"I hope they made it," she said, simple and quiet.

"Your brothers?"

She nodded. "I hope they got patched up and were able to move on."

"I'm sure they're fine."

She arched a brow at Luke as they stepped up onto the front stoop of the Hen House and through the door. She wasn't sure, but for now she was content to imagine they would be fine, just as Luke said.

The Hen House was more or less as they'd left it when Eden ran off to join the drive, only cleaner. She thanked heaven for that small miracle, because at the moment, she was far too tired to sweep and tidy and scrub.

"I just want to take off my boots, crawl into bed, and sleep for a week," she groaned as she plodded through the main room and into the bedroom.

She emphasized her point by flopping, face first, onto the bed, arms spread to the sides. Luke chuckled as he came up behind her and sat on the side of the bed. She listened as his shoes fell to the floor, one by one, then to the swish of fabric as he pulled his shirt up over his head. They had washed and changed into clean clothes before going to supper, so she didn't have to worry about him getting dirt all over the floor.

Luke stood, and Eden closed her eyes and began to drift into sleep. A minute or so later, she felt tugging on her feet as he unlaced and pulled off her boots.

"Mmm, thank you, sweetie," she sighed, twisting her head to the side, but leaving her arms stretched out.

"You're welcome, dear," Luke replied.

The deep, hungry growl in his voice popped Eden's eyes open. Prickles shivered along her skin as he reached up the folds of her skirt to peel off her stockings. The brush of his fingertips along the flesh of her thighs left trails of fire in their wake. She sighed at the sensation as a delicious ache pooled in her core. It grew in a hurry once her stockings were both off and Luke continued to rake his fingernails up and down her thighs.

"Oh my," was all she could manage before Luke took hold of the hem of her skirt and drew it up over her waist.

She gasped as he reached around to tug the drawstring of her drawers loose, then to yank them down and off over her feet, exposing her naked backside to him.

"Luke Chance, what are you—"

Her question ended in a gasp as he grabbed hold of her ankles and spread her legs wide apart. A powerful shiver ran through her at the feeling of being so exposed to him, and while lying in such a yielding pose. Why, with her on her stomach, legs spread, arms at the side like that, he could do anything to her. He could—

The bed creaked as Luke climbed between her legs. The naked flesh of his sides rubbed against her thighs as he slid himself on top of and between her.

"Dear Lord, you're naked," she panted.

The hard spear of him settled against all the things that counted between her legs as he growled, "Yep," against the back of her ear.

Forget exhaustion. Forget sorrow and regrets. She wiggled her hips and backside against him, aching to be filled. He rewarded her with an intake of breath and a groan that sizzled along her skin. She wanted to be naked too, for her clothes to disappear so she could feel his skin, hot and tender against hers. But not as much as she wanted to feel him insi—

All thought left her with a wanton moan as he thrust inside of her. He felt so good and so tight sheathed in her that she had a hard time catching her breath. She'd forgotten how big he was and how his size and power made her feel as though she were being stretched to the limit in all the best ways. She tilted her hips up into his thrusts, rocking back against him with each one and crying out with the pleasure they brought.

Mad as their coupling was, the coil of pleasure pulled tighter and tighter inside of her with his thrusts. He paused long enough to shift their position, drawing her hips up off the bed so that he could plunge deeper. He reached to twine his fingers through hers as she balanced on her arms, closing her eyes and losing herself to the sensation of him around her, inside of her. His heat, his weight, his thrusts were all divine.

The urgent tension inside of her squeezed so tight that she couldn't stand it anymore. She rolled her weight to one arm, twisted his hand in hers so that she held it from behind, then brought it under her and around the folds of her skirt. As soon as his fingers made contact with the hot, hard nub between her legs, she cried out with the goodness of it.

Luke, ever the fast learner, caught on and brushed against it as he continued to thrust into her with increasing urgency. His masculine grunts of pleasure pitched higher and higher as he came closer to finding release. Eden beat him to it. She gasped as the coil inside of her broke free into vibrant pulses of pleasure. Her whole body sang in reaction, her limbs going weak as pleasure carried her away, and with it, a happiness more potent than anything she'd known.

A moment later, before her orgasm had ridden itself out, Luke reached his climax. He let out a long, loud groan as his body tensed and released, his life and his heat surging into her. The force of their combined expansion left them both limp and spent, in a heavy tangle of arms and legs, dress and bedclothes, on top of the bed. But Eden didn't mind. She was more than happy to lay there panting as all energy left her.

At length, Luke shifted, rolling to the side and drawing into his arms. "Well, shoot. I was hoping to get your clothes all the way off before I got to the point where I couldn't stop myself."

Eden giggled. She reached for the fastenings of her skirt. "Sweetheart, we've got all the time in the world to be naked together." She proved her point by shimmying out of her skirt, then undoing and tossing aside her bodice, corset, and chemise.

Luke hummed in appreciation. He started to move to pull back the bedclothes, but stopped and fixed her with a serious stare. "You sure it was all right to do it that way? You know, behind-like."

Lord, how she loved him. She loved his sweetness and his innocence, and she loved his strength and his command. She was the luckiest woman alive to have stumbled into his arms. No, not stumbled, taken a chance. He was her second chance.

"Honey," she drawled, flickering an eyebrow at him with a look that she was much too tired to follow up on. "I've seen some books. There are all sorts of ways to do it, front, back, and sideways. We'll have to work our way through each one."

He laughed as they crawled under the covers and settled for sleep. "Doesn't sound much like work to me."

Really, it didn't. In fact, she had a feeling the two of them would enjoy getting into mischief of all sorts of kinds—in bed and out—for the rest of their days.

Epilogue

"Boy, you two didn't waste much time, did you?" Cody stepped up onto the porch of Luke and Eden's completed house, Travis following, as Eden and Luke sat on the wicker bench watching the sunset. The air had a late-autumn nip in it, but Eden barely felt it. She had a thick shawl wrapped around her shoulders and Luke snuggled up to her side.

"What are you talking about?" Luke asked. The satisfied grin he wore belied the fact that he knew just what rumors had reached Cody's ears. He reached across to rub Eden's stomach.

Cody snorted and shook his head at the two of them. "Word every which way around here is that it's a good thing they built so many rooms in this house, because you're gonna need them before next spring."

"Really?" Luke grinned at Eden. She, in turn, winked at him over her shoulder.

"Did I forget to tell you, sweetie?" she teased him. "I'm in the family way."

"You don't say," Luke played along, all pretend innocence. "How'd that happen?"

"Well, it probably has something to do with the way—"

"Don't." Travis held up both hands to stop them. He held a folded piece of paper in one. "There are some things I don't need to know."

Eden giggled and snuggled closer to Luke. As far as she was concerned, life couldn't possibly be better. She knew full well how she'd ended up with child, and so did Luke. Like she'd thought all along, he was a fast learner. Especially since they practiced frequently.

"What's that you've got?" Luke nodded to the paper in Travis's hand.

Travis and Cody both turned serious. Cody sank to sit in the rocking chair across from the bench, and Travis leaned against the porch railing and stared at the paper. It was a clipping from a newspaper.

He glance up at Eden with an uncertain look, then said, "Theophilus Gunn's been keeping an eye out for any mention of—" He cleared his throat. "—Of anything having to do with a certain gang back East."

Eden sat straighter, her heart beating double-time. Luke gripped her shoulder to keep her steady. "Did he find anything?"

Travis nodded and handed the newspaper clipping over to her.

"I don't understand how that man knows everything," Cody muttered. "It's like he's got a sixth sense or something."

"He doesn't have a sixth sense," Travis scoffed. "He's just observant."

"How'd he know about what happened out there on the drive anyhow?" Cody asked.

"I told him," Luke answered with a shrug.

"You what?"

Eden ignored the exchange. Luke had told her about his conversation with Mr. Gunn weeks ago.

"Gunn has a way of being there when you need someone to talk to," Luke said.

"Ain't that the truth," Travis agreed.

"You just find yourself telling him things, and then he gives you all the advice you'll ever need."

Travis hummed. Cody shook his head, baffled. Eden was too busy scanning the newspaper clipping to pay them much mind.

"Braden was arrested," she said softly.

"Honey, I'm sorry." Luke pulled her closer and hugged her from the side.

Eden barely noticed that too. "No, there's more." She read and reread the article—short though it was—to make sure she read it right. "Bert turned him in."

"What?" Luke leaned into her, reading the article over her shoulder. "Well I'll be," he murmured as he read.

"Seems one of your brothers, at least, refused to return to a life of crime," Travis said. Evidently, he'd read the article too.

Eden let out a breath and relaxed against the bench and Luke's arm. She closed her eyes and said a quick prayer of thanks. "At least two of us got away." And maybe more. The article didn't say anything about her cousins—even though she'd scanned the entire page for mention of Ted—but at least it hadn't mentioned them being arrested either.

"This is good news," Luke said, giving Eden a squeeze.

"It is." She smiled up at him, adding a light kiss for good measure.

"But one thing." Luke's expression dropped to a scowl.

"What?" She arched a brow.

"This doesn't mean we're naming our baby any name that starts with a 'B.'"

Eden laughed out loud. "*Hell* no," she agreed. They shared another kiss.

"And guess what?" Cody burst in.

Eden snuggled closer to Luke as he tightened his arms around her. "What?"

"Mr. Garrett, Mrs. Piedmont, and Mrs. Evans have finally agreed to send for a bride for me."

Cody finished his announcement, and Travis hid his face in his hand and shook his head.

After everything she'd learned about Cody in the last few months, Eden was inclined to agree with Travis's assessment of the situation. All she said aloud, though, was "Really?"

"Yep," Cody answered with pride. "Apparently, a Miss Wendy Weatherford will be coming out on the train in three weeks." He sent a smug look to Travis.

"Do you know her?" Luke asked Eden.

Eden furrowed her brow and shrugged. "No. She must be new at Hurst Home."

"She's a seamstress," Cody added.

Travis peeked up from where he was still hiding his face in his palm. "Well, at least the town needs a seamstress."

Cody sniffed and scowled. To Luke and Eden, he said, "Travis doesn't think I'm ready for marriage."

"You're not," Travis said.

"He thinks I lack maturity and commitment," Cody went on, ignoring him.

"You do." Travis shook his head.

Eden glanced to Luke. She could see her own thoughts on the matter reflected in his expression. Travis was right. Cody was in for a shock. But neither of them were about to tell him that.

"Well," Eden said as diplomatically as possible. "I wish you as much happiness as Luke and I have found."

Cody grinned like a cat and stood. "That's exactly what I'm hoping for. Come on, Travis. Let's go check out the house Howard said I could have." He pointed to the mostly-finished building next door to Luke and Eden's house. "We're gonna be neighbors."

Without waiting for a reaction, Cody tugged on Travis's sleeve, and the two of them clamored off the porch to take a look at what would be Cody's house. Travis sent Luke and Eden a wary look as they left.

"I wonder how that'll work out," Luke said, resting his cheek against the top of Eden's head.

"I have no idea." She chuckled, then scanned the article Mr. Gunn had clipped for them. With a sigh, she added, "At least I know they're alive."

"That's something," Luke agreed.

Eden twisted to hug him. She loved the way they fit so well together, loved that they could enjoy these peaceful moments together, man and wife. "All I can do is pray that they get second chances, just like I did."

"You and me both," he said. She let out a breath and closed her eyes, resting her head on his shoulder. "I love you, Eden Chance, and I will until the day I die and beyond."

"And I love you that much and more."

It was all she needed to say, all she'd ever needed.

I hope you've enjoyed getting to know Haskell, Wyoming a little better and falling in love with Eden and Luke in *His Dangerous Bride*. Remember, reviews are always appreciated. There's much more Haskell to come, sooner than you might think. After all, Cody asked for Josephine, Virginia, and Charlie to send for a bride for him. Wendy certainly is…surprising, and between you and me, it's a good thing that Travis is there at the train station when she arrives. Just sayin'. You can read all about it in *His Bewildering Bride*, coming soon!

About the Author

I hope you have enjoyed *His Dangerous Bride*. If you'd like to be the first to learn about when the new series comes out and more, please sign up for my newsletter here: http://eepurl.com/RQ-KX And remember, Read it, Review it, Share it! For a complete list of works by Merry Farmer with links, please visit http://wp.me/P5ttjb-14F.

Merry Farmer is an award-winning novelist who lives in suburban Philadelphia with her two cats, Butterfly and Torpedo. She has been writing since she was ten years old and realized one day that she didn't have to wait for the teacher to assign a creative writing project to write something. It was the best day of her life. She then went on to earn not one but two degrees in History so that she would always have something to write about. Her books have topped the Amazon and iBooks charts and have been named finalists in the prestigious RONE and Rom Com Reader's Crown awards.

You can email her at merryfarmer20@yahoo.com or follow her on Twitter @merryfarmer20.
Merry also has a blog, http://merryfarmer.net,
and a Facebook page,
www.facebook.com/merryfarmerauthor

Acknowledgements

I owe a huge debt of gratitude to my awesome beta-readers, Caroline Lee, Margaret Breashears, and Jolene Stewart, for their suggestions and advice. And a big, big thanks to my editor, Cissie Patterson, for doing an outstanding job, as always, and for leaving hilarious comments throughout the manuscript. Also, a big round of applause for my marketing and promo team, Sara Benedict and Jessica Valliere.

And a special thank you to the Pioneer Hearts group! Do you love Western Historical Romance? Wanna come play with us? Become a member at https://www.facebook.com/groups/pioneerhearts/

Other Series by Merry Farmer

The Noble Hearts Trilogy
(Medieval Romance)

Montana Romance
(Historical Western Romance – 1890s)

Hot on the Trail
(Oregon Trail Romance – 1860s)

**The Brides of Paradise Ranch –
Spicy and Sweet Versions**
(Wyoming Western Historical Romance – 1870s)

Willow: Bride of Pennsylvania
(Part of the American Mail-Order Brides series)

Second Chances
(contemporary romance)

The Advisor
(Part of The Fabulous Dalton Boys trilogy)

New Church Inspiration
(Historical Inspirational Romance – 1880s)

Grace's Moon
(Science Fiction)

Made in the USA
San Bernardino, CA
27 April 2017